Shattered

Just where does one cross the point of no return?

When a sweet, intelligent twenty-five year old with un-diagnosed Asperser and PTSD seeks help from a ruthless, unscrupulous, sadistic therapist, she shatters his psyche and throws him into a suicidal depression. Her crude attempt to pick up the pieces -- enslaving him and subjecting him to unethical, unsanctioned, experiments -- ignores the lines of consent and the responsibilities of a Dominant. -- Inspired by a true story.

"The work ... unfolds with the assured touch of a bestsell-ing mainstream author, seducing us into the lives of people with needs and agendas that find wings in the dark. Only an author familiar with this landscape could peel back these layers of psychological complexity without flinching and without dramatic compromise ... Prepare to submit to this reading experience, which will mark you with its narrative power.

> Larry Brooks, USA Today bestselling author of
> *Darkness Bound* and *Bait and Switch*

As a FemDom, I.G. Frederick knows first hand the beauty of symbiotic D/s relationships filled with love. As an observer she sees the many ways BDSM turns ugly. She writes about abusive and tragic interactions as Korin I. Dushayl.

I.G. Frederick trades words for cash, specializing in erotic and transgressive fiction and poetry since 2001. Her erotic short 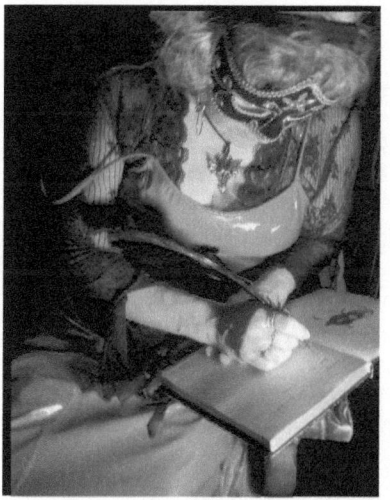 stories appeared in Hustler Fantasies, Forum, Foreplay, and Desire Presents, as well as electronic, audio, and print anthologies. Her novels receive high praise from readers, critics, and other authors.

Ms. Frederick, owns the man she adores who although dominant in the rest of his life, demonstrates his love by serving as her submissive.

http://transgressivewriter.com

SHATTERED

Just where do you cross the point of no return?

Korin I. Dushayl

Author of *Broken* and *Playing With Dolls*

Shattered
Second Edition
© **2011 by I.G. Frederick**

ISBN: 978-1-937471-93-4

Pussy Cat Press
http://pussycatpress.com/publisher.html/
P.O. Box 19764
Portland OR 97280

First published in the U.S.A. 2008

Dedication

To christian: you will always have a place in my heart. Wherever you land, I hope that you find the love you deserve and the peace that has eluded you for so long.

Chapter One

Zachary Smith lined all the brochure holders up with each other on the counter next to the window that protected the receptionist from the patients. Then, he straightened each stack of brochures in each holder. He rearranged the magazines on the oak coffee table, putting them in date order and set them on top of each the other so just the title of the magazine appeared beneath the magazine on top of it. He lined up the oak arm chairs so they each stood one inch away from the wall. As he reached out to straighten the metal-framed print of a still life with fruit and flowers that hung over the chairs, the receptionist's window slid open. "Mr. Smith, could you please sit down. Dr. Richards will be with you shortly, but you did arrive almost a half hour before your appointment." The frumpy woman wearing a dress covered in tiny white daisies stared at Zachary until he sat down. As soon as she closed the window again, he rose to his feet and fixed the picture. He stared at the clock over the window and watched the black second hand tick its way around the white face inside the white plastic frame.

The door next to the window opened and a beautiful woman, almost as tall as he, stepped out with a clipboard in her elegantly manicured hands. Slender, he guessed she couldn't weigh more than a hundred and twenty-five pounds, she had hair blacker than night that hung down and brushed her shoulders. She wore a tailored blue suit with a white blouse.

"Mr. Smith?"

Zachary looked up into her piercing green eyes and nodded.

"I'm Dr. Jessica Richards." She extended a hand and Zachary just stared at it, unwilling to sully such beauty, even if she permitted it. Eventually she withdrew it. "Why don't you come into my office, Mr. Smith."

Zachary followed the woman down a hallway of closed doors. She walked into one near the end and pointed to two upholstered armchairs under the window. Between them, a small metal table held a box of tissues, a water pitcher, and two glasses upside down on a tray. To get to a chair, he had to pass an oak desk which had a laptop computer, a pile of file folders, and a chrome lamp on it. Another chair, this one with wheels and levers to adjust the back and seat, sat in front of the desk.

Sitting in an armchair, Zachary put his hands in his lap. Then he put them next to his thighs. Then he sat on them.

"Let me just confirm some basic information, if I can." Dr. Richards held the top sheet off the clipboard and read from the page underneath. "You're twenty-five years old, you dropped out of the university in the middle of last term, and you live in Humboldt Park."

Zachary nodded.

"And why are you here at the clinic?" Zachary moved his hands between his thighs. "Zachary, or do you prefer Zach?" "Zachary," he whispered. "Ummm, could I see someone else?" How could he explain what he needed to this beautiful woman? He had never had a female therapist before, never mind one so stunning.

"Perhaps, you could give me a chance first?" Dr. Richards turned over one of the glasses and filled it half full of water from the pitcher. "We've only just met."

She pushed the glass toward Zachary; he took it and emptied it in one swallow.

"According to the forms you filled out, you have problems with anxiety and depression, you don't do well in social situations, and all this has resulted in your dropping out of college where you majored in philosophy for the past three years. Is that correct?"

Zachary nodded. He wanted nothing more than to escape the confines of her office. He felt as if the room had gotten smaller since he sat down.

"Also, according to this, you've never held a job for longer than six weeks."

Zachary lowered his eyes and moved his hands back to his lap, clutching them together.

"Zachary, would you be more comfortable if I stood behind you while we talked?"

Zachary nodded his head. Maybe if he didn't have to look at her, he could explain his problems.

Z

When he left the clinic, Zachary tried to decide where to go. Already late for work, he didn't know if he should rush to get to the grocery store or just give it up and go home. If Ramona had the shift, she would just let him stay late to make up for the time. As long as he got all the shelves stocked and the expired dairy products out of the coolers, she didn't care too much about when he showed up. But Stella had already given him two warnings and had told him one more late arrival and she would ask Mr. Larson to fire him.

The bus pulling up to the stop in front of campus as Zachary approached would take him to the Treasure Island. He decided to go to work and hope for the best.

"Zachary," Ramona called when he pushed open the swinging door to the back room. "Don't punch in." She grabbed his arm and pulled him behind a stack of empty milk crates. "Stella's complained to Mr. Larson and you're on report. I'll fill out your timecard when you're done with your shift and you can tell him you forgot to punch in. Go ahead and take care of the dairy case. The pallets can wait until the store clears out a little, after the evening rush."

Zachary put on his apron, tied it around his waist, and grabbed one of the empty milk crates. He spent an hour pulling products that had passed their sell-by dates, replacing them with fresher items, and straightening the rows of milk cartons, cottage cheese containers, and butter boxes. He probably should call the clinic and tell them he wouldn't return for the appointment the frumpy receptionist had scheduled for him on Thursday. Dr. Richards seemed nice enough, but she asked so many questions he didn't know how to answer.

Z

Jessica ushered Zachary into her office for the third time. This one puzzled her. Usually she could diagnose a patient's primary and secondary issues by the end of the first visit. Although she thought she had determined Zachary's primary diagnosis, something beyond that had impacted his mental health but she could not determine what. She wondered if she might use him to test the intriguing research trickling out of Siberia.

"I have some information for you today that might prove useful." Jessica crossed her legs and folded her hands together. She still couldn't get Zachary to look at her. "Have you ever heard of Asperger's Syndrome?"

He shook his head.

"It's a very mild form of autism, and I believe that's why you have difficulty succeeding in social environments." Jessica hadn't known that much about it herself until she started comparing the behaviors commonly found among patients with Zachary's symptoms. Jessica handed him a brochure and read the paragraph she had circled in her copy. "Typically those who suffer from Asperger's are deficient in social skills, have difficulty with transitions or changes, develop obsessive routines, are preoccupied with particular subjects of interest, cannot read nonverbal cues such as facial expressions, tone of voice, and body language, and are overly sensitive to sounds, tastes, smells, and sights. Often, like yourself, they are extremely intelligent, but they don't always find productive ways to demonstrate that intelligence."

Zachary clutched his copy of the brochure, nodding at each point Jessica brought up. "Can I get a prescription then?"

"I'm afraid it's not that simple. No drug therapy is available for AS itself, although we can try medication to help with your depression and anxiety problems."

He frowned and crumpled the brochure in his hands. "Doesn't help anything to put a name on it, then."

"I disagree. If we work together we can help you develop the social skills you need to function in most environments. I think you can even reach a point where you could have some semblance of a normal life. However, most patients with Asperger's don't experience your level of social dysfunction. I believe very strongly that something else is causing your depression and anxiety and until we know what that is, I can't really design an effective treatment program."

Zachary scowled. In the three hours she had spent with him, he had hadn't smiled once. His expressions ranged from inscrutable to downright angry.

Chapter Two

Jessica met Zachary at the front door of the building and ushered him upstairs to her office. She had closed his official file, claiming that he had stopped keeping his appointments, and only saw him after the other interns and supervisors left for the evening. Her supervisor would never approve of using a patient to test out Speransky's therapy methods, but Jessica thought Zachary might be the perfect candidate.

Sitting at her desk, Jessica glanced at her notes from the previous session. "Now, Zachary, I would like you to tell me more about the year you spent with your uncle in New Jersey."

Zachary sat in one of the two armchairs, facing the window. Since he seemed more comfortable speaking to her if he didn't have to look at her, Jessica had gotten into the habit of turning the chair away before ushering him in for his appointments.

"Nothing much to tell. My father ran out on my mom. She couldn't take care of me so she sent me to stay with her brother-in- law until she got back on her feet." Zachary tapped his foot in a rapid movement that Jessica had come to realize meant the question caused him discomfort.

"How did you get along with your uncle?"

"Okay, I guess." The tapping accelerated. "Did he have

children of his own?" Zachary pulled his long legs up into the chair and wrapped his arms around his knees. "Yeah."

"And, how did you get along with them?" "Okay, I guess." "Did your uncle treat his own children differently than he treated you?" Jessica rose and stood behind Zachary's chair, stroking his long blond hair. If she was still seeing Zachary under supervision, she would get reprimanded for the physical contact. But, often she could use touch to calm him enough so he could verbalize his thoughts.

"He was a mean, ruthless, vicious, judgmental prick who seemed to get his kicks out of making me feel like I wasn't up to par with his own children. He kept pointing out how different and awkward I was. He always made it clear that I wasn't part of the family. He called me Zach even though I asked him not to." Zachary trembled like a heroin addict deep in withdrawal.

Jessica debated interrupting him, but he seemed so close to touching on something epiphanic. Despite the agitation his memories caused, she hated to stop him. She rubbed his shoulders, taken aback by the tension in his muscles.

"He had four kids, all of whom slowly became infected with his attitude of seeing me as some undesirable intruder into their home." Zachary fingers balled up into fists and his knuckles turned white. "I slept in a closet on the carpet with only a thin blanket. I couldn't wear my clothes to bed so I was always cold. He punished me for my lack of social skills by making me eat in the kitchen by myself while everyone else ate in the dining room. He would hit me so hard with his belt on my bare ass, he often broke skin. I had bruises on my arms from where he grabbed me, on my shins from where he kicked me."

Jessica leaned over the back of the chair and wrapped her arms across Zachary's chest. He grabbed onto her forearms, clinging to her.

She rested her cheek on the top of his head, offering comfort in her embrace to assuage the pain his memories would generate. "What else did he do to you, Zachary?"

His chest heaved and a sob escaped that sounded like a banshee's cry.

Jessica felt wet tears dripping onto her arm, but with Zachary on the verge of breakthrough, she kept pushing. "What else did he do to you, Zachary?"

"No, don't touch me." Zachary tore her arms from his chest and hurled himself under her desk.

His violence startled her and she had to grab the chair to keep from losing her balance, but Jessica wasn't willing to give up when he was so close to acknowledging what had happened in his childhood. She took a deep breath and walked over to the desk, leaned against the wall, and slid down so she squatted where he could see her face. "What else did he do to you, Zachary?"

Zachary curled up in a ball with this back toward her. His sobs shook his body so violently, Jessica worried he would hurt himself against the desk. Afraid she had pushed him too far, she crawled toward him, slowly put her arm under the desk and touched his hair. He didn't resist, but he didn't change position either. Nor did his sobbing abate.

"I think we've covered as much ground as we can today, Zachary." Jessica kept her voice soft and soothing. She had to calm him down, she couldn't have him leaving her office in this state. "Why don't you come out from under the desk. We don't need to talk any more during this session."

He didn't react.

"Please come out from under there, Zachary. You'll feel better if you do." Jessica slid her hand from Zachary's hair along his arm until she reached his fingers. She tried to undo his fist enough so she could get a hold of his hand. Although he resisted at first, eventually his fingers relaxed and he allowed her to take his hand and tug on it.

When he crawled out from underneath the desk, Jessica

pulled him into her arms and let him sob, shaking, with his face pressed against her shoulder. She stroked his hair and rocked him back and forth until he calmed down.

When his shaking stopped, she breathed a deep sigh of relief, but she didn't try to coax him to his feet until he stopped crying. Then she led him over to the chair and the box of tissues next to it. He blew his nose several times but ended up choking and she had to pat him on the back. Finally she got him to drink a glass of water and his hand remained steady while he did.

"Will you be okay going home?" He swallowed and nodded.

Z

Zachary missed his next two appointments and didn't answer his phone when Jessica tried to call him. After his second no-show, she debated whether she should call the police and have them check up on him. But of all her patients, he seemed the most likely candidate to test the Siberian research. One advantage he offered was his lack of a social network. If he disappeared for a few weeks, no one would notice. Creating a police file could create obstacles.

Jessica decided to pay Zachary a visit. She discovered he lived in a run-down structure that looked more like a hotel than an apartment building. The elevator had an "Out of Order" sign hanging from it and the stairs stank of urine. She debated about leaving, but in her six months at the clinic no other patient had presented such a perfect opportunity. Since she had read the rumors about Russian scientists in Siberia using whipping therapy to treat everything from drug addiction to depression, Jessica had wanted to do her own research. She knew she could never get anyone at the university or the clinic to endorse any kind of study and needed a patient she could persuade to let her try it.

After climbing the stairs, holding a handkerchief over her nose, Jessica had to bang on Zachary's door for almost ten minutes before he opened it. He reeked of sweat and unwashed clothing, several days of beard covered his face, his skin appeared pasty white, and he and looked like he had lost ten pounds.

"What?" He shaded his eyes from the light of the bare bulb in the hallway ceiling.

"You missed your appointment today."

"Ummm, I thought that was tomorrow. Sorry. I'll call and reschedule." He stepped back and pushed the door closed.

Jessica stuck her foot in the door. "You also missed your first appointment this week." She observed his emaciated form and bloodshot blue eyes. "When's the last time you ate?"

Zachary shrugged.

She pushed her way past him into the room despite his efforts to block her. Torn blue jeans and worn sweatshirts hung over two metal folding chairs. Empty take-out containers from a grocery store deli covered the card table that sat against one wall and the shelf that held a small microwave and a toaster oven. The unmade bed looked as if Zachary had climbed out of it to answer the door. A pile of magazines, the top one pornographic, sat next to the bed. Instead of a closet, the room had a rack attached to the wall next to the door. Another door, open next to the shelf, led to the bathroom. Even from this angle, Jessica could see how tiny it was.

"How long since you've left this room?" Jessica crossed her arms under her breasts, disgusted by the depths to which he had sunk.

Zachary shrugged.

"Have you gone anywhere since your last appointment?" He already had problems with late arrivals at work.

He shook his head.

"So you've missed work?"

"They left a message this morning. I'm fired."

Jessica ran her hand through her hair, pretending concern. Losing his job eliminated Zachary's only other connection to anyone other than herself. "How do you plan to pay your rent?"

Zachary shrugged.

Jessica walked over to the shelf and opened the mini-frig under it. It contained a half-full quart of milk that she could see through the plastic had curdled and a package of cheddar cheese that had mold growing on it. She closed the door. "Go take a shower and then we'll go get something to eat. You look like you haven't had any food in a week."

Zachary stared at her.

"Now!" She couldn't experiment on an emaciated patient.

He shuffled toward the bathroom and closed the door. Jessica heard water running. She pulled open the top drawer of the pressboard dresser next to the bed. In it she found white briefs and socks, folded precisely and stacked in neat piles, that appeared clean. She pushed the drawer closed and waited for Zachary to emerge from the bathroom, hair wet and sticking out in every direction, a towel wrapped around his waist. He removed a pair of briefs from the top drawer, a pair of jeans from the bottom one, and returned to the bathroom. When he reemerged, he wore the jeans and had combed his hair. He extracted a blue tee shirt with a picture of John Lennon on it from the second drawer and pulled it on over his head. When he had put on socks and shoes, he stood in front of Jessica.

"Good. Let's go." Reluctant to leave her car in the neighborhood where Zachary lived, Jessica drove him to a White Castle, the only restaurant nearby, and parked in the lot.

He followed her obediently into the brightly lit, gleaming white, tile interior. Afraid too much stimulation would make him bolt, Jessica had Zachary sit at a corner table facing the wall while she ordered a sack of ten Slyders, a large order of fries, and an orange Crush. She asked for it to go in case he couldn't finish it. Food in hand, she slid into the molded plastic booth facing him.

Reaching into the bag, she pulled out a paper-wrapped hamburger, opened it, and set it in front of him. The scent of onions and steamed meat wafted up from between the bun and turned her stomach. You couldn't get much more plebeian in Chicago than White Castle. Jessica set the cardboard container of crinkle-cut fries on the paper next to the hamburger. Zachary took one and chewed on it. Then he picked up the hamburger and devoured it in two bites. Jessica pulled another from the bag and pushed the soft drink closer to his hand. In ten minutes he had consumed everything in the bag and slurped down the soda.

Z

Jessica flipped through the pages of handwritten notes in Zachary's file. Since she started seeing him after hours, she had stopped dictating her reports for the transcriptionist. Although he had come to the clinic with serious problems, he had still functioned. He managed to find a job each time someone "let him go." He paid his rent and ate regularly. And he never missed a therapy appointment.

Five months later, since she had forced him to remember the sexual abuse he suffered as a child, he missed more appointments than he made, couldn't find work, rarely ate, and faced eviction from his room. Jessica had tried escitalopram, venlafaxine, clomipramine, benzodiazepines, and alprazolam. He had allergic reactions to all but one combination and the medications he could tolerate had no apparent effect. Although she could try other SSRI/benzodiazepines combinations, Jessica debated whether any drug therapy would help Zachary. And, since she saw him outside the auspices of her internship, she had to send him to a free clinic in Evanston to get his prescriptions filled.

He had reached the point where he needed institutional commitment to survive. To treat him, a therapist would need to experiment with various drug combinations over time while staff monitored his reaction, made sure he ate adequately, and prevented him from sleeping twenty hours a day. She hoped he would find any other option. including experimental therapy, preferable.

Chapter Three

"Have you eaten today, Zachary?" After he followed her up the stairs, Dr. Richards ushered him through the doorway of the inner sanctum, one hand on her hip.

He pulled the plugs out of his ears and stashed his Walkman in his jacket pocket. When he passed her, always so impeccably dressed, he became self conscious about his ragged jeans, less-than-clean shirt, and unshaven face. He dragged his hands through his hair then wiped the grease off on his shirt. In Dr. Richard's office he could smell the lavender and vanilla that permeated her hair and skin. As usual, she wore a straight, above-the-knee skirt, and matching jacket, over a silky-looking blouse. Her shoes seemed uncomfortable, but they made her shapely calves appear very sexy. He cringed that he had allowed himself to think that.

"You didn't answer my question, Zachary." Her voice came from behind his chair. Unfortunately, since he no longer bathed regularly, Dr. Richards didn't touch him like she once did. But dragging himself to her office twice a week had become a major accomplishment. The building manager kept threatening to throw him out on the street, he rarely remembered to eat, and shaving and bathing just didn't seem important any more. "What question?"

"Have you eaten today?" She put her hands on the back

of his chair and he wished she would play with his hair like she once did.

He shrugged. "What day is it?"

Dr. Richards took a long, deep breath. "You haven't responded to any treatment options I've tried, Zachary. Right now, I see two choices." She paused as if waiting for him to say something and kept going when he didn't. "One option is to commit you to an institution. Doctors could try various drug therapies until they found something that helped you manage your depression."

Zachary shrugged. At least he wouldn't have to worry about getting evicted. But then he remembered what happened the last time he had gotten himself locked up. His hands shook so he shoved them in his pockets.

"That also would alleviate your immediate financial predicament, since once I started commitment proceedings, a social worker can try to get you made a ward of the state." Again she waited. "But, I'm not sure drug therapy will help you get through this crisis and I'm not even sure I can find an available bed for you."

Really, he didn't think of his situation as a crisis. He'd already lost maybe twenty pounds. If he just locked himself up in his room and resisted Dr. Richards' attempt to feed him, probably he would starve in a week or two. Then he wouldn't have any problems, she wouldn't have to worry about him, and the guards at the institution couldn't get their hands on him.

"I would like to try an alternative form of therapy, something that hasn't received any kind of endorsement from the American medical community."

"Sure." Although locking himself in his room presented the easiest solution for him, he doubted that Dr. Richards would allow him to do that.

"You don't even know what it is."

Zachary shrugged. It had to beat getting put away.

"You would have to sign this." Dr. Richards handed him a three- page document, stapled at the top.

Zachary tried to read the words, but the letters jumped around on the page. He took the proffered pen and scratched his name on the bottom of the last page. When he lifted pen and paper, Dr. Richards accepted them back.

"This is a confidentiality agreement to protect us both. In it you agree not to discuss your treatment with anyone, to not sue me if it's not effective, and you waive your right to compensation for any damages." Dr. Richards stepped around and sat on the window sill, forcing Zachary to look at her. "Do you understand what I just said?"

"I can't talk about my treatment." Zachary pulled the neck of his shirt over his mouth.

"I suppose that's enough for now. You need to go home, bathe, put on clean clothes if you have any, and return here by six o'clock tomorrow evening. Can you do that?"

Zachary shrugged.

"Do you have any food or any money for food?" He shook his head. Dr. Richards stepped away and returned with a ten-dollar bill in her hand. She gave it to him. "You need to use this to buy some food. I want you back here clean and fed tomorrow evening. Can you do that for me, Zachary?"

"I'll try," he whispered. If he didn't, she would probably come drag him out of his room again.

Standing on the sidewalk outside the clinic, Zachary clutched the ten-dollar bill inside his pocket. He knew he didn't have any clean clothing at home and he could use some of the money to do laundry. But that seemed like too much effort. He wandered in the direction of the bus stop, but his transit pass had expired weeks ago and he didn't have any change for the fare. Walking toward home, the smell of gyros wafted out from a restaurant entrance.

He went inside and spent seven of his ten dollars on the daily special. The plate came with meat, pita, humus, tabouli, and tzatziki, sauce. Only the garlic of the spicy sauce registered with his consciousness, but his stomach didn't growl or hurt when he left the restaurant.

The following evening, Zachary arrived at the clinic at half past six and found the door locked. Usually Dr. Richards waited for him in the lobby and let him in. Putting one hand on either side of his eyes, he peered through the glass, but could see no one. He looked around for a pay phone, then wondered if anyone would answer if he called. Not knowing what else to do, he sat down on the edge of the concrete planter in front of the building and watched for anyone to emerge. Dark clouds roiled in the sky and threatened to unload their burden at any moment. The wind kicked up and Zachary shivered.

Ten minutes later, Dr. Richards came out of the building and headed toward the parking lot. Zachary followed her. Halfway down the center aisle she whirled around. She paused and took a deep breath.

"Zachary, you startled me. I'd given up on you." She rummaged in her purse and took out a set of keys. "Come on."

He followed her to a blue Mustang convertible. She climbed into the driver's seat and waited. Zachary shuffled around to the passenger side and folded himself onto the seat, minimizing the contact he had with the leather upholstery. He had bathed and found a pair of jeans that wouldn't have fit a week ago stuffed under his bed. They didn't stink when he shoved his nose in the crotch. He had combined that with a tee shirt that had gotten lost in his dresser and a pair of clean socks that he hadn't worn before because they had holes in the heels. He felt he didn't belong in such a nice car.

Dr. Richards drove through rush hour traffic for a good forty- five minutes. He thought they had left the city behind, but he really couldn't tell. They traveled through streets of shops and houses with cars everywhere. Lightening cracked and the dark clouds dumped buckets of rain on them. Dr. Richards turned on her windshield wipers and headlights. Zachary wanted to get out of the car at the stop lights and run away, but he didn't know where to go. The thought of ending up in a hospital, where guards could abuse him again kept him in the car.

By the time Dr. Richards pulled into a garage attached to a two- story house with mint green siding and forest green trim, Zachary had curled up into a ball leaning against the car door, his thighs pulled up to his chest, his arms wrapped around his shins, his head buried between his knees. She stepped out of the car while the door to the garage cranked closed behind them. Zachary didn't move.

The car door opened and he almost fell out onto the concrete floor.

"Come inside, Zachary." Dr. Richards extended a hand with long fingers and nails painted dark burgundy.

Slowly, he uncurled into a standing position outside the car, careful to avoid touching Dr. Richards' hand or any other part of her. He followed her to a doorway and into a kitchen. A naked woman stood at the stove. The pert little blonde dropped to her knees in front of Dr. Richards, leaned down, and planted her lips on first one foot and then the other.

Dr. Richards lifted the woman's head by her hair and kissed her. "I'm going to take this boy downstairs for a while. Can dinner keep?"

"Yes, Mistress," the blonde girl said.

Zachary stared at one then the other of them. He wiped the back of his hand across his eyes, but the blonde girl still knelt in front of Dr. Richards, her big, luscious tits pointing straight at his knees.

"This way, Zachary." Dr. Richards walked through the kitchen, opened a door, and led him down a flight of stairs. At the bottom, she stopped at another door. "Do you agree that conventional therapy hasn't worked for you?"

Zachary nodded.

"Do you agree that you need something drastic to break you out of this episode?"

Zachary shrugged. Not really, he'd rather just wallow in his depression until he drifted beyond her reach, but he couldn't tell her that.

"Are you willing to try an unproven, alternative therapy rather than hospitalization?"

"I guess." He didn't think she would take no for an answer.

Dr. Richards opened the door. In the unfinished basement, an X-shaped cross leaned up against one wall and a sofa with a black and red afghan draped over it sat against the other. A metal cage stood in the corner, with a padded table in the middle of the room. Some smaller tables had an assortment of nasty looking tools on them.

"Some researchers have used pain to effectively treat depression. Pain causes the release of endorphins which can reduce anxiety and stimulate your sense of well-being. They can also reduce serotonin levels, but given that you're sleeping excessively, I don't believe that will cause you any problems. Do you understand what I'm saying?"

Zachary shrugged.

"I would like to try treating you with pain to see if that brings you any relief. Do you agree to this form of treatment?"

Zachary stared at her. "Not like I've got much to lose."

"Then, take off your clothes."

He pulled the tee shirt over his head, looked around and set it on the padded table. Kicking off his shoes, he picked up one leg, then the other, and pulled off his socks. He stood with his hands jammed in his pocket while she stared at him.

"I need access to all of your skin, Zachary."

He turned his back to her, unzipped his jeans, and slid

them down over his hips. He added those to the pile on the table and held his hands over his privates.

Dr. Richards took two leather cuffs from one of the small tables and buckled them around his wrists without moving his arms. She led him over to the cross, lifted one hand, and hooked the cuff to the top of the arm. He resisted when she reached for the other hand, but she dug those long finger-nails into his arm until he let her bring it up and fasten it to the other side of the cross. Then she put more cuffs around his ankles and hooked them to the bottom of the arms.

He strained to see her over his shoulder, watching her pick up a four-foot long, braided, whip. *What have I gotten myself into?*

Chapter Four

The first blow didn't sting; it felt more like a caress. She kept hitting him, though. And she struck harder and harder. The whip cut into his flesh. He clenched his fists and struggled against the cuffs holding his wrists. She hit him so hard, he screamed. Then she hit him again. He wanted to escape the torment. The whip cracked, it bit into his ass, his back, his shoulders, then it cracked again. Crack, pain, scream. Crack, pain scream. His world became the whip, the whip became his world.

He no longer stood on his feet, his weight hanging from his wrists. His muscles let go and his mind floated inside his body. He still heard the whip sing through the air and the click of Dr. Richard's heels on the concrete floor when she moved. He felt the heat of her body when she stepped closer. He could smell her vanilla skin and the leather of the cuffs holding him upright. He tasted the salt of his tears in his mouth. His skin burned from the welts she had raised with the whip. But his mind was free.

The whizzing of the whip stopped and he felt soft hands caress his bruised flesh. He heard her sweet voice, but couldn't distinguish the words. He just took comfort in the sound penetrating the euphoria that fogged his brain. With a click, his wrists dropped to his side. He expected to fall to the floor, but a shoulder propped him up. He stumbled with

Dr. Richards over to the sofa. She sat him down and wrapped her arms around him. His lips sought her mouth and when he found it, he kissed her hard, only dazedly aware of the boldness that required. She let him suck hungrily on her tongue.

The scent of musk overpowered him and he longed to suck on more than just a tongue. He kissed his way down the soft skin of Dr. Richard's neck. She unbuttoned her blouse and let him pull her succulent breast above her bra cup so he could take her hard nipple in his mouth. He moaned softly. He had never touched a woman's breast before, at least not since he could remember.

Dr. Richards grabbed a fistful of his hair and pulled his head lower. She scooted her skirt up her thighs and guided his face between her legs. Her scent intoxicated him. He inhaled deeply, unable to get enough. Urged by her grip on his hair, he pushed his face forward and stuck out his tongue. She tasted heavenly. He wanted more. He licked and sucked the sweet juices, pressing his face tighter against the exquisite softness. He tried to recall what he had read in the porn magazines.

The only thing he could remember was the need to find her clit. He searched with his tongue until found a hooded nub at the top of her slit. When he pressed the flat of his tongue there, she rewarded him by trembling against him and giving him even more juices to lick up. He concentrated on the tasty little nub and sucking up the nectar his attention to it released.

When Dr. Richards pulled his face away, he grabbed onto her thighs, trying to stay in the heaven he had found. She yanked on his hair until he relented and withdrew, not because her tugging hurt. No pain could compare to the stinging fire on his back. But, he knew he needed to please her and give her what she wanted. Much to his delight, she pulled him back up into her arms and let him rest his head against her shoulder and nuzzle her neck with his nose. He shivered and she pulled the thick, warm afghan around him.

"How are you feeling?"

He wanted to tell her about the overwhelming and profound emotions that assaulted his senses, but he couldn't get his lips to form words. After weeks of near catatonia, the euphoria of sensation inebriated him and he floated in a sea of ecstasy. He managed to make a sound in his throat that he hoped would signal his happiness, but it came out more like a squeak than a contented sigh. Dr. Richards stroked his hair and he snuggled closer.

"I'm going to let you sleep in the cage for tonight, you'll be safe in there, no one can touch you."

Zachary made the noise in his throat again, but this time it came out less squeaky and more like a kitten's purr.

Dr. Richard's stood up and led Zachary to a door at the far end of the room. She opened it to reveal a sink, toilet, and shower. Despite her watching him, and a raging erection, he managed to relieve himself. After he washed his hands, Dr. Richards took him to the cage in the corner. She opened the door, waited until he crawled in, and handed him the afghan. Then she closed the door and fastened a large padlock through the hasp. Zachary curled up on the two-inch-thick vinyl-covered foam pad with the afghan around him and watched her legs walk away from him. With a click, the lights disappeared and he heard the door close.

For a moment, memories of his uncle's closet assaulted him and he could feel the panic starting in his stomach. But here the thick mat separated him from the floor, the heavy afghan kept him warm, and she had promised he would be safe and that no one could touch him. He could still taste Dr. Richard's musk in his mouth and that helped him push away the memories from his childhood.

Licking his lips, remembering the wonderful taste and feel of her against his lips, he stroked himself until he came with a jerk. Although he wanted to clean up the mess he had made, he only had the afghan and didn't want to get that dirty. He drifted off to sleep with his fist still wrapped around his now flaccid penis.

Z

Pain roused Zachary, but he had no idea how long he had slept. His right shoulder hurt where it pressed against the pad at the bottom of the cage and the stripes across his back and rear burned. The rough wool of the afghan chafed his tender skin, but if he removed it, he shivered with cold.

He sat up, but then his backside hurt. Curling up on his left side, he tried to use the pain of the welts on his back to find the euphoria he had experienced the night before. Although he couldn't reach the exhilaration he had known when Dr. Richards let him lick her, he did manage to find a rush that made the pain pleasant instead of intolerable. He drifted off to sleep again.

Z

Jessica extracted the key to Zachary's room from his pants pocket and sent Dora there with a large duffle bag and a suitcase. Given that he had already fallen six weeks behind in his rent, the manager wouldn't need much of an excuse to confiscate Zachary's things. Although she hadn't gotten the impression that he owned much of value, Jessica decided retrieving his personal effects would prevent him from resisting her decision to keep him in her dungeon for a while.

She drove to the clinic to finish cleaning out her desk. At the previous day's staff meeting, she had passed along her files to those who would continue at the clinic after she left. Now, only Zachary's file was still locked in her desk. Jessica fiddled with the key, thinking about the lovely office she had selected to house her own practice. On Monday, her post-doctoral work completed and her licensing secured, she would start her day there instead.

Unlocking the drawer, she pulled out Zachary's file and flipped through the pages. Despite his signature on the confidentiality agreement, if he established a strong relationship with another therapist could she trust him to not reveal details of her alternative therapeutic methods? Since he signed it while incapacitated by mental illness, the document wouldn't hold up in court. Jessica closed her eyes. Even if, given the results, she could justify the whipping, she had to admit she crossed the line when she succumbed to her need and let him lick her.

She opened her eyes. One whipping wouldn't cure Zachary. The Russians recommended thirty sessions of sixty strokes. Zachary would stay at her house until she verified the effectiveness of the Siberian Therapy long term. For her own protection, she probably should break him to make him dependent on her and less likely to share details. Jessica slipped his file into her briefcase.

Before shutting off her laptop, Jessica checked her e-mail. Professor Lawrence complained that she hadn't visited Tom for the last three weeks and Roger had reported that he hadn't seen her either. Jessica called the University and made an appointment to see Professor Lawrence that afternoon.

Z

The naked blonde brought him food. Plain oatmeal and water -- the best thing he had tasted in months. The water had a cold, refreshing feel as it slid down his parched throat. Even though he could tell the oatmeal had no sugar or honey, it had a sweet taste. He chewed each spoonful, relishing the flavor and texture of the individual pieces against his tongue.

"Thank you, Ma'am." He handed her the bowl through the bars of his cage. "Do you think I could use the restroom?"

"How are you feeling this morning?"

"Better, much better. Thank you, Ma'am."

"You should only call, Mistress Ma'am'. You can call me Dora."

Zachary nodded. He remembered the blonde had called Dr. Richards Mistress when they had arrived at her home. He wondered how long since she had brought him down to this dungeon.

Miss Dora unlocked his cage and let him crawl out. He followed her to the small bathroom.

"There's a clean towel hanging from the rack. Go ahead and take a shower. When you're done, use your towel to tidy up the bathroom and to clean up the mess you made by the cage."

Zachary felt the heat rising to cheeks, but the blonde took his bowl and cup and left the basement. After relieving himself, he found soap and shampoo in the small shower stall in one corner of the bathroom. He washed his hair three times and scrubbed every inch of his skin with the bar of soap. Clean felt good, despite the pain the water and soap elicited from his welts. After rinsing himself, he used the hand-held showerhead to rinse the walls and door of the shower.

Stepping out, he dried off, cringing when the terry cloth touched his raw skin. Then he used the towel to mop up the water he had dripped on the floor and the dried semen from the puddle he had left just outside the bars of the cage. He didn't know what to do with the dirty towel, so he snuck a peak outside the door of the dungeon. Another door on the other side of the stairs led to a laundry room and he dropped the towel in a pile of others on the floor. For some reason the other pile -- tee shirts and socks -- looked familiar. He lifted a black shirt with a picture of John Lennon on the chest. Another had a quote from Nietzsche: "In the consciousness of the truth he has perceived, man now sees everywhere only the awfulness or the absurdity of existence . . . and loathing seizes him." Both shirts stank. He dropped the shirts and returned to the bathroom to wash his hands again.

Zachary tried in vain to remember when he had brought his clothing over to Dr. Richards' house. He wanted to go upstairs and ask Miss Dora, but she hadn't told him what to do when he finished his shower. Returning to the cage, he retrieved the afghan, wrapped it around his shoulders, and curled up in a corner of the sofa.

Chapter Five

Driving across campus, Jessica received a call from Felicia on her cell phone. "The Professor has changed your meeting to his home office." The girl disconnected the call before Jessica could argue. Squealing her tires, she made a u-turn in front of the psych building and headed out toward Sheridan Drive.

When Felicia opened the door, Jessica stomped past her and marched into the Professor's office. "We're through. I've gotten my dissertation published, I have my degree, and starting Monday I have my own practice -- no affiliation with the University. You no longer have any hold over me." She had to clench her fists behind her back to keep from spitting the words in his face.

"You might have difficulty getting patients if they find this when they Google your name on the Internet." Professor Lawrence pointed a remote at the television inside the cherrywood cabinet against the wall. The screen filled with a picture of Jessica, naked, strapped to the dentist's chair in the dungeon downstairs. Gloved hands inserted needles into her breasts, painted brown with iodine wipes.

Jessica sank into the chair, her knees no longer able to offer any support. The Professor pushed a few buttons on the remote and the picture changed to Jessica hanging naked from a cross, her breasts and belly covered with red welts from the flogger and a giant red dildo protruding from between her legs. Jessica put one hand to her mouth and dug her fingernails into the palm of the other to avoid bursting into tears.

"Would you like to see more?"

Jessica swallowed and shook her head. "You worm."

"What was that, Dr. Richards?" He paused. When she didn't respond, he continued. "I make these for, shall we say, insurance purposes." He pushed a button, the television went blank, and he set the remote on the edge of his desk. "As long as you continue to meet weekly with Professors Ross and Smythe, these videos will remain locked in my vault."

Jessica took a deep breath. If he tried to take her down she would not go alone. "I want more money."

"What?" The startled look on his face, strengthened her resolve.

"If you put those pictures on the Internet, I'll have no incentive to keep my mouth shut. I'm sure I can persuade at least one of your other victims, perhaps more, to expose your abuse. Together, we can convince the chancellor that you're more of a liability than an asset to the University." Jessica crossed her legs and rested her hands lightly on the arms of her chair trying to demonstrate more calm than she felt.

"You forget, my dear, that you're the only student currently in service who didn't beg for the opportunity to wear my collar." He folded his hands together on his blotter. "I doubt you'll find anyone to corroborate your claims."

Jessica's stomach churned and bile burned her throat, but she refused to back down. She remembered his many former students who had moved far away from the Chicago area. "Tom and Roger pay you six hundred for each visit. Right now, I do all the work and you still collect more than half the money. I will inform them that if they want to continue seeing me, they need to pay me when I visit. Once a month, I will give you fifteen percent as a commission."

Professor Lawrence's eyes widened, slightly. "I suppose I could persuade Professors Ross and Smythe to serve someone else -- especially if I offered them a discount to try her."

Jessica took a deep breath to calm the shakiness she felt. "When I cut off your collar, I also severed the control you held over me. I continued taking care of Tom and Roger to make my internship and post-doctoral work easier on both of us. I have no desire for a public confrontation. But, if it comes to that, you have a hell of a lot more to lose than I, whether or not anyone believes me." Jessica leaned slightly forward. "I will keep quiet and give Tom and Roger what they want because you can still facilitate my career advancement. I expect you to recommend me as a therapist and make sure numerous affluent patients get referred my way."

"I might consider allowing you to continue as Professors Ross' and Smythe's Dominatrix for twenty percent. If you make your own arrangements with them, that will take less effort on my part. But if you want referrals for affluent patients you will need to pay commissions."

"Fine, I'll pay you twenty percent of what I receive from Tom and Roger and twenty percent of one month's billing for any patients who give me your name when they make their first appointments." Jessica rose and placed her palms flat on the Professor's desk. "But, these are business relationships. I no longer serve you in *any* way." She turned and walked out, overwhelmed by her need to remove herself from his presence before she broke down.

In the car, Jessica's hands shook so hard, she had to pull over once she rounded the first turn taking her out of sight of the Professor's house. As soon as she put the car into park, she burst into tears. Covering her mouth with her hands, she sobbed, her shoulders shaking. Despite her assertions, the thought of anyone seeing the video of her submitting to the Professor and his colleagues mortified her. She would do almost anything to prevent that. The threats she made meant nothing. She knew she could never really expose Professor Lawrence. He probably knew that as well. But the Professor had bullied and abused her for the better part of three years. If she didn't draw a line now, it would never end.

Her sobs subsided, but Jessica still felt shaky. Knowing she couldn't let either Zachary or Dora see her in this condition, Jessica managed to maneuver her car to the Chase Café. Inside she ordered a pot of chamomile, hoping that would help her calm down. She booted up her laptop and logged onto the Internet long enough to set up a free e-mail account. From theladyonthelake@yahoo.com, she sent e-mails to both Tom and Roger informing them that from now on they would contact her directly about when they hoped to serve her and that she would expect her full payment in cash when she arrived at their homes. They no longer would communicate with Professor Lawrence about any aspect of their service to her. She copied the Professor on both e-mails and sent him a separate e-mail with her office phone number, address, and URL for referrals.

As she sipped the fragrant tea, Jessica breathed deeply and let her muscles relax. She pulled Zachary's folder out of her briefcase and rifled through it in an effort to push thoughts of the Professor and his submissive clients from her mind. Extreme physical pain should have jolted Zachary from his catatonia, at least temporarily. She called Dora.

"How's the boy?"

"He seems better, Mistress. He ate what I brought him, bathed when I told him to, and made no attempt to come upstairs. He did ask for a book so I gave him a couple of novels to choose from. I think he's halfway through one of them."

Jessica smiled. A good start.

"The boy ate?"

"Yes, Mistress. I only gave him plain oatmeal for breakfast and a peanut butter sandwich for lunch, since you didn't leave any specific instructions. I've never seen anyone enjoy something so vile so much."

Jessica laughed. "Just because you hate peanut butter, my dear, doesn't mean everyone else does."

Returning home an hour later, Jessica went to check on Zachary as soon as Dora finished greeting her. She found him curled up in the cage, reading a paperback copy of Neverwhere. He looked up, saw her, and crawled out of the cage to kneel at her feet. "Miss Dora said I couldn't use the furniture without permission, so I thought it best if I stayed in the cage until you got home."

"How are you feeling?" Jessica resisted an urge to stroke the boy's head.

"Much better, Dr. Richards. Thank you so much. I've regained some clarity and I seem to have regained a bit of an appetite."

"You may call me, Mistress."

"Thanks. I'd like that." He smiled and Jessica enjoyed seeing the brightness in his blue eyes. But she couldn't let that dissuade her from the tactics she knew were necessary. She turned and walked over the sofa. When he didn't follow, she snapped her fingers and pointed at the floor by her feet.

Zachary stood up, walked over, and sat down on the floor next to her.

She grabbed a fistful of his hair and spoke into his ear. "You'll stand if I tell you to. Otherwise you crawl on all fours like the dog you are."

"Yes, Ma'am."

"That's 'Yes, Mistress.' "

"Yes, Mistress." He stared at her with a puzzled look in his blue eyes.

"You'll look at me if and when I tell you that you may. Otherwise, keep your eyes down at my feet where you belong."

Zachary looked startled, but he lowered his eyes. "Yes, Mistress."

"In this house, you don't so much as go to the bathroom without permission." She yanked his head back further, but he avoided looking at her. Training him wouldn't be difficult. "Do you understand?"

"Yes, Mistress."

She released his hair and left him sitting there while she walked over to a cabinet that hung on the wall near the bathroom. She returned with a handful of leather which she piled on the sofa. First she held a jacket up for him to insert his arms into. When he got his hands inside the sleeves, he picked them up and examined the closed ends with straps hanging from them.

"Stand up." Jessica turned him around and buckled the jacket closed in the back, then pulled his arms tight across his chest and fastened the straps behind his back. She took the straps dangling from the bottom of the jacket's front and brought them between his legs to buckle to the back of the jacket. She pulled the hood over his head, made sure the eye, nose, and mouth holes lined up, and laced it up in the back. When she had the hood secure, she snapped the blindfold into place, inserted a plastic gag in his mouth and fastened the two snaps that would hold that in place.

The sight of him encased in leather with his backside and genitals exposed aroused Jessica. She wanted very much to take him with her strap-on, but worried that would traumatize him with memories of the abuse he had suffered as a child. With one hand, she caressed his bruised rear. Then she ran her fingernails across the welts. He got hard and Jessica laughed. Unable to resist the temptation, figuring one kind of pain would work as well as another, she led him over to the padded table, helped him get up on it, then laid him flat. She ran one sharp fingernail along the length of his hard-on, and it jerked. Jessica grabbed a cloth bag full of clothes pins and applied them to the boy's scrotum. He moaned, about the only sound he could make with his mouth full of gag.

Jessica ran a hand over the ends of the clothes pins. He squirmed. She whipped his genitals with a small leather flogger until a strangled scream emerged from behind the gag.

"Mistress, dinner is ready." Dora knelt in the doorway.

Jessica yanked the clothespins off Zachary's scrotum, ignoring the muffled howling. She helped him off the table and lead him over to the cross and secured him using the d-rings attached to the ends of the sleeves and the collar. She added ankle cuffs which she clipped to the bottom of the cross.

"You've got something to eat here before you can even think about dinner." Jessica walked over to Dora and grabbed her by the hair. She dragged the girl over to the sofa and stood in front of her. Dora ran her hands up the outside of Jessica's thighs and hooked her thumbs into the waistband of her pantyhose. She dragged the nylons down Jessica's thighs, letting her fingers stray across Jessica's heated flesh.

When Dora had the hose down to her knees, Jessica dropped onto the sofa. She allowed Dora to pull both her panties and the stockings off, then opened her legs.

Chapter Six

Zachary measured time by how badly he needed to empty his bladder before someone led him to the bathroom and let him relieve himself. He hung on the cross, he curled up in the cage, he swung from the ceiling tied with rope. Confinement blended into pain blended into bondage. The hard round, rubber gag stayed in his mouth except when someone took it out and let him drink water or made him eat vile nutrition bars that tasted awful and that he could barely chew.

Mistress never allowed him to sleep. Whatever position she put him in, she found ways to torment him so he stayed awake. She had covered every inch of his skin with bruises, welts, and pricks. Once she told him he stank, took off the hood, and threw him in the shower. Even the cold water stung and touching himself with the soap brought tears to his eyes.

He just wanted to sleep. Even if no one ever let him eat real food again, if he could only curl up and sleep for a few days...

"What are you?" She poked at his wounded skin with a fingernail. If he didn't have the gag in his mouth, he would have screamed.

He knew the answer she wanted, even though he couldn't say the word. Pushing himself up onto his knees, he banged his head on the top of the cage. But then he could bring his hands up in front of his chest, curling his fingers together in the shape of paws.

"Good boy." She patted the top of his head.

He moved as close as he could to the bars of the cage to maximize his contact with her wonderfully soft hand grateful for once it offered no pain.

"If I let you out of the cage, can I count on you to behave like a good little puppy?"

He nodded his head as vigorously as he could in the confines of the cage. Metal scraped against metal and the hasp released from the lock which came away from the cage. The door opened and he crawled out on his hands and knees. He could smell vanilla nearby and he raised his head, sniffing. When he found her, he rubbed against her legs, hoping she would pet instead of strike him.

Her steps walked away from him. "Heel boy."

He scurried to keep next to her leg, hoping she wouldn't lead him into anything. When she stopped, he rubbed his hooded head against her leg. Fingers fumbled at the leather around his mouth and unsnapped the pieces holding the rubber gag between his lips.

When it pulled out of his mouth, he tried to say "Oh, thank you, Mistress," but his tongue stumbled over the words. He followed her leg down to find her foot and covered her shoes with kisses. Then he moved to her other foot. He sensed her sit down, and her foot lifted off the floor. He sucked on the spiked heel and licked the leather of the top. She moved her foot and loosened the heel. Hoping he read her signal correctly, he removed the shoe and turned his attention to her stockinged foot. He used his thumbs to massage the heel and ball while caressing the tops and toes with his lips.

She rewarded him with a little pleasurable moan. He removed the other shoe and gave that foot equal attention. Her feet tasted good. Not as wonderful as the sweet honey between her legs, but lovely enough that he could have kissed and licked her feet for hours. The silky softness made it easy to forget the pain on his skin.

He felt hands on the back of his head and although the hood became looser, he continued to devote his attention to her feet. When she pulled them away from him, he whimpered. But then she lifted the hood from his head and he tried to open his eyes. Even the dim light hurt and he covered his eyes with his hands. Her fingers pried them away. He wrapped his arms around her legs and clung to them. She stroked his hair, pushing it away from his face.

"I don't think you can survive on your own, boy." Her soft voice sounded so pleasant after such a long time when only the sound of leather and wood hitting skin penetrated his hood. "I've decided to keep you as a pet, a slave. You'll serve me and I'll take care of you."

The touch of her hand in his hair calmed him and he leaned against her legs. "Yes, Mistress. Thank you, Mistress."

She buckled a leather dog collar around his neck. "This is a temporary collar. You'll wear it while you learn the protocols you're expected to follow and how I wish you to serve me."

He felt the collar with two fingers. It had a D-ring on the side opposite the buckle and metal spikes encircling it. "Yes, Mistress. Thank you, Mistress."

"You'll eat out of the dishes there." She pointed to a mat next to the bathroom door. On it he saw two ceramic bowls. One had water in it and the other held something light brown with dark brown spots. "You'll sleep in the cage, and the rest of your time you will spend taking care of me, my house, and my slave, Dora."

"Yes, Mistress. Thank you, Mistress." "You may eat now." Zachary crawled over to the dishes where the scent of oatmeal accosted him. He used his lips to suck up chunks of the cereal that had raisins and milk mixed in and then chewed

slowly savoring the sweetness of the fruit against the delicious oats. He sucked up wonderfully cool mouthfuls of
water, enjoying the sensation of the liquid sliding down his
throat. When he had licked both bowls dry, he crawled back
over to the sofa and put his head on his Mistress' knee.

"Whenever I haven't assigned you a task, the way you let
me know you're available to serve me is to assume the position." She took a fistful of hair and guided him back onto his
knees so his rear rested on his heels. "Open your legs, put
your hands on your thighs, palms up."

He complied.

"Straighten your back, but keep your eyes down."

Zachary squirmed to follow her instructions. Although
the concrete floor felt cold against his shins, his posture had
a grace that lent dignity to the humility of the position at his
Mistress' knees. He found it comforting.

"Good." She patted on the top of his head. "Unless you
have duties to perform or are in your cage, you will assume
this position. Make sure I can see you, but never try to get
my attention in any other way unless there's some kind of
emergency. Do you understand?"

"Yes, Mistress. Thank you, Mistress."

"You may go take a shower. Come find me upstairs when
you're done."

"Yes, Mistress. Thank you, Mistress." Zachary planted a
kiss on each of her feet then rose and headed toward the bathroom. "Never turn your back on your Mistress like that." He
stopped in midstride. "Always back away with head bowed
and then turn around when you're out of the room."

"Yes, Mistress. Thank you, Mistress." He dropped back
to his hands and knees, crawled back to her, and kissed her
feet again. When he rose, he kept his chin on his chest, and
walked backwards toward the bathroom, arm extended to
feel for the wall, looking at her through his lashes.

She rewarded him with a smile before he turned back

through the door and closed it. A moment later it opened.

"You're never permitted to close a door inside the house unless you're instructed to do so.

"Yes, Mistress. Thank you, Mistress."

"When your Mistress enters a room, you always drop to your knees until you discover what she wants of you."

He lowered himself to the floor. "Yes, Mistress. Thank you, Mistress."

"That's better. You may take off the collar to bathe." She turned and headed for the door that led to the stairs.

Although showering still hurt, now the bruises and welts seemed like badges of honor and the pain brought catharsis and peace. When he had dried off, shaved, and brushed his teeth, he made his way up the stairs for the first time since Dr. Richards -- Mistress -- had brought him home. He wondered how long ago, but then decided it didn't matter. He found his Mistress sitting on a leather sofa in her living room. She had changed into jeans and a tee shirt and had a magazine in her hands. Miss Dora knelt on the floor besides her, massaging and kissing her feet.

Zachary assumed the position in the middle of the floor where his Mistress could see him. Although he kept his eyes down, he couldn't help staring at her through his lashes. Her long dark hair framed her pale face. She had crossed one long leg over the other, and even under a loose-fitting tee shirt he could see the shape of her breasts. He remembered how wonderful they had felt in his mouth and to his embarrassment, his cock hardened.

"Dora, go online and order a CB-3000." Mistress turned a page in her magazine.

"Yes, Mistress. Thank you, Mistress." Miss Dora backed out of the room and Zachary wondered if she tasted as good as their Mistress.

Mistress snapped her fingers and pointed to her feet. Zachary crawled up to the sofa and took one delicate foot in his hands. Her skin, free of hosiery, felt so soft he rubbed his cheek against it. Then he concentrated on massaging the heels and balls. He wanted to do better than Miss Dora so Mistress would require him to attend to her feet. But when Miss Dora returned, Mistress let her pick up where she had left off. Zachary stayed on his knees, waiting.

Chapter Seven

Three days later, Zachary learned what a CB-3000 was. When the package arrived, Mistress took out several pieces of plastic. She handed him a flat ring, about two inches in diameter and instructed him to secure it behind his scrotum. He opened the ring, placed it against his skin and pubes, and closed it. Then Mistress gave him a transparent, tubular cage. When he took it from her, it dawned on him what she intended to do. His hand shook as he slipped the cage around his penis. It barely fit -- an erection would hurt like hell.

While he held the cage in place, Mistress stuck plastic pins from the ring to the tube. The last pin had a small hole through which she put the hasp of a brass padlock. When she snapped it closed, he just stared at himself encased in polycarbonate, locked up so he couldn't touch it. Mistress took the key and slipped it onto a chain which she fastened around her neck. A tear crept down his cheek.

After cleaning up from several messy tries, Zachary gave up trying to stand up when urinating. He learned to pee sitting down. He woke up every morning in pain, the cage clamping down on his erection. But, gradually he became used to the CB and accepted it as he had learned to accept living naked, spending long periods of time on his knees, and eating out of a dish on the floor.

Miss Dora taught him how to cook for Mistress and do

all the household chores. Zachary made step-by-step lists for each instruction Dora gave him, filling the pages of a spiral-bound notebook. Every time she or Mistress found fault with something he did, he would record in detail what he had done wrong. Eventually, Miss Dora allowed him to spend his days cleaning, doing laundry, and preparing meals rather than locking him in the cage when she left for school.

Zachary liked having precise directives for how to spend his days and only floundered when he completed the list of tasks Miss Dora gave him before she or Mistress returned home. When Mistress realized he had time on his hands, she allowed him to spend up to an hour a day on the Internet. Although he visited some of the philosophy chat rooms where he used to hang out, he used most of that time to research sites discussing protocols and rituals for slaves. Each time Zachary incorporated a new ritual into their routine that earned him a pat on his head or a "good boy" from his Mistress, he added it to his notebook.

After he had lived in her home for almost six months, Mistress instructed him and Miss Dora to prepare for guests the following night. Zachary spent most of the day cleaning the house, paying special attention to every detail. When he finished, he helped Miss Dora put coconut cookies and small kebabs with pieces of fresh pineapple, papaya, and mango she had prepared onto plates along with chocolate truffles from Marshall Field's.

About seven in the evening, an older woman, no taller than Miss Dora but much heavier, arrived with a tall skinny man who wore a dark grey raincoat. Mistress said nothing about putting on his clothing and Miss Dora did nothing to hide her nakedness when they arrived. Zachary wanted to run down to the dungeon, rather than be exposed to strangers, but Mistress had not dismissed him. The man removed his coat. Underneath he only wore a double strand of chain links around his neck and a plastic CB similar to the one Zachary had on. Zachary let out his breath and took the man's coat to hang in the front closet. He decided if Mistress wanted him naked in front of these people, he had to accept it.

The man removed the woman's leather jacket and handed it to Zachary. She wore a black polyester men's shirt tucked into black jeans. Her nails had no color on them, she smelled only of soap, and she didn't even wear lipstick. While Zachary put the heavy jacket over a wooden hangar, the man got on his knees and assumed the position. Mistress gave the older woman, whom she called Alyssa, a big hug.

"Thanks so much for joining us this evening," Mistress said.

"Oh, I'm delighted you included us." Alyssa patted the man's head and followed Mistress into the living room. Zachary, Miss Dora, and the man crawled after her.

"Would you like something to drink?" Mistress pointed to the sofa.

Alyssa took a seat and the man knelt at her feet. "I'd love a glass of wine."

Mistress turned to Miss Dora. "Bring her a glass of Chablis."

"Yes, Mistress." Miss Dora backed out of the room and returned with a full wineglass. She handed it to Alyssa.

Mistress stood in front of the coffee table and snapped her fingers at Zachary. He crawled to her side and assumed the position. She draped stainless steel links, a single row, around Zachary's neck, the two ends dangling on either side. "I place this collar on your neck as an instrument of my ownership and control. It symbolizes submission of your body and your mind to me as well as my responsibilities as your owner. Do you willingly accept my collar?"

Zachary frowned. Why did she ask him? He didn't want to make a decision about anything, preferring to let Mistress do that for him. "Yes, Mistress. Thank you, Mistress." He knew that answer worked for anything.

She pulled the two ends together, pulled another link through them, and closed it with a small pair of pliers. "Now that I have placed it on my property, this collar may never be removed except by me."

"Yes, Mistress. Thank you, Mistress."

She pulled his head back by his hair and kissed him on the forehead. Zachary closed his eyes and smiled, glad to have delivered the appropriate answers without coaching. Mistress always rewarded him when she didn't need to tell him what she wanted. Mistress sat down next to Alyssa and nodded to Miss Dora.

"Zachary," Miss Dora whispered and backed out of the room. He followed her lead and brought one hand up to feel the links while they walked into the kitchen. Miss Dora handed him the plates with cookies and fruit kebabs. She picked up two smaller, empty plates and the truffles and led him back to the living room.

They set the full plates on the table and Miss Dora handed empty plates to Mistress and Alyssa. After she put a kebab and a truffle on her plate, Mistress snapped her fingers and pointed at her feet. Zachary turned to Miss Dora, but she nodded her head toward Mistress. Grateful to be the one summoned, Zachary crawled toward Mistress and gently removed her shoe. He could hear her talking with Alyssa, but he concentrated on massaging her feet, occasionally pausing to kiss her toes, rather than listen to what they said.

He could feel the metal links resting on his collarbone. No one had ever given him jewelry before. Zachary rubbed Mistress' heel with his thumbs the way she liked. He thought about the collar and the plastic CB. Both confirmed that someone cared enough about him to take responsibility for him and that he belonged here at Mistress' feet. He nodded his head. Yes, he belonged here.

Z

A week after she fastened the collar around his neck, Mistress had Zachary get dressed and drove him into the city. He had only left her house twice since she brought him home, once to see a dentist and have his teeth cleaned and the other time for a physical. He tried to remember how long since those events had taken place, but he found it very difficult to keep track of the days and weeks as they passed.

Mistress parked on a side street and they walked several blocks along sidewalks that reminded him of where he lived before Mistress took him home to take care of him. The storefronts needed paint and they all had roll-down barriers that were tucked up for the day and apartments above the shops. Mistress stood in front of a place called BodyMod until Zachary opened the door for her. Inside Zachary saw glass cases full of barbells, navel rings, nostril studs, ear plugs, and more. Large paper panels, framed in black metal, along one wall displayed hundreds of bright-colored flash tattoo art. A sign behind the register listed age and consent requirements.

"The boy here would like a tattoo," Mistress told the girl behind the counter.

The woman had half-inch wide, hollow, bone earlets in both lobes, as well as having her bottom lip, one eyebrow, and her right nostril pierced. Two small beads rested at the base of her neck, apparently connected under her skin. She had a flowery tattoo that started at her wrists and disappeared under the sleeves of her Violent Femmes T- shirt.

She shoved a piece of paper at Zachary. "You need to fill this out and show me your identification. Are you using flash or do you have your own art?"

Zachary looked at Mistress. She produced a piece of paper from her pocket. It had a picture of a gold circle divided into three sections with a gold curved line dividing each one. The inside of each section was black, except for a hole in the center of each.

"Where?" The woman smiled as if she understood Mistress' secret.

"On his right hip." "Yes, Ma'am." She turned to Zachary. "You need to fill out this form without your Mistress' assistance." She handed him a blue ballpoint pen.

Zachary read the paper entitled "Consent to Application of Tattoo Release and Waiver of All Claims." It said: "I acknowledge by signing this writing that I have been given the full opportunity to ask any and all questions which I might have about obtaining a tattoo from BodyMod, Ltd., and that all of my questions have been answered to my full and total satisfaction. I specifically acknowledge that I have been advised of the facts and matters set forth below, and I agree as follows:"

Even though he had many questions he would like answered, Zachary couldn't imagine asking them. He scribbled his initials at the beginning of each line acknowledging that he was not pregnant; had no communicable diseases; was over 21; would assume the risk of any allergic reaction to the dyes, pigments, or processes used in his tattoo; that he needed to care for his tattoo to avoid infection; had received instructions for the proper care of his tattoo; understood the tattoo was permanent; that he had chosen on his own to get a tattoo; and that he released and forever discharged and held harmless BodyMod, Ltd., from any claims, damages, or legal actions connected in any way with his tattoo. Then he filled in his name, his birth date, and signed the form. He passed it to Mistress who added her address and phone number.

The woman took his identification card and disappeared through a doorway.

"This is the BDSM emblem." Mistress held the piece of paper up in front of Zachary. "Submissives wear it on the right, Dominants on the left." She ran one finger along the lines separating the three crescent shapes. "These represent the BDSM threesome of bondage and discipline, domination and submission, and sadism and masochism."

"Yes, Mistress. Thank you, Mistress." Zachary had never particularly wanted to get a tattoo. But, if Mistress required that of him, he would accept it. He thought the emblem rather pretty. He wondered why each section had a blank spot, but knew Mistress would explain it if he needed to know.

The woman with all the body art returned and held out a piece of tracing paper with the emblem drawn on it to Mistress. "This okay? I've used this art before and I think it's a little nicer than that one." She pointed to the paper Mistress still held.

"That will do just fine." Mistress tucked her paper back into her coat pocket.

"This way, then." The woman led them to the small room in the back of the shop. "Take off your pants, boy."

Zachary complied and she patted the padded table in the center of the room. He climbed up onto it and lay on his left side. She scrubbed his hip and he could smell antiseptic. Then, she positioned the paper above his hip while Mistress pointed to where she wanted it to go. When Mistress nodded, the woman pressed it against his skin.

When she lifted the paper, it left a purple imprint of the emblem on his hip. She dipped a tool into a tiny plastic container of black ink. He heard a buzzing and she touched his hip. The pain made him open his eyes wider, but it didn't compare to what Mistress inflicted with her whip. He took in deep breaths to manage the discomfort.

Z

Like Dora, Zachary needed very little discipline. His desire to please Jessica always seemed genuine and he responded with a grateful look when she patted him on the head or let him worship her feet. Jessica still gave him klonopin to keep his anxiety under control. About once or twice a month when he exhibited signs of depression -- lack of appetite, sleeping longer every day, irritability, and inattention to his chores -- Jessica flogged him. Striping his back with the leather always turned her on, so she allowed Zachary to satisfy her orally after she beat him. But Jessica preferred sex with Dora and except as an anti- depressant for Zachary, Jessica saved her time in the dungeon for Dora as well.

After he finished cleaning up from supper one evening, Jessica observed Zachary watching Dora worship her feet. Since Zachary took care of most of the household chores, when she returned home from work Dora had more time to devote to Jessica's personal needs. Jessica watched in dismay as Zachary, sitting in the position to let her know he had finished his chores, scowled at his sister slave. He clenched and unclenched his fists, frightening Jessica.

Although she had broken him, in addition to the occasional fits of depression, Zachary still suffered from Aspergers, Post-Traumatic Stress Disorder, and anxiety. Any one of those could cause him to lose control and become violent. Jessica's eyes widened and she suddenly felt cold. Dora sometimes got home an hour or more before Jessica did, she realized. She pulled Dora into her arms. Had she put her love in jeopardy by bringing Zachary into their home?

While she held Dora and caressed her hair, Zachary's scowl turned darker and his knuckles whitened. Jessica laughed in relief, realizing Zachary was probably just jealous. After all, Dora slept in Jessica's bed, got most of Jessica's sexual attention, and even had more time in the dungeon with her Mistress.

"Go get my laptop," she instructed Zachary. He scurried from the room and returned to kneel in front of her presenting the computer on his upturned palms. Jessica patted him on the head and put the computer on her lap while Dora returned to pleasuring her feet. She needed to find options to allow Zachary to spend more time serving her personally. Surfing the web, she thought about sending him to cosmetology school so he could learn to cut her hair, wax her legs, and do her nails. But any program she looked at required a personal interview and expected students to interact well with their peers and the public. Zachary would never succeed in that type of environment.

She did find an online massage therapy program. Although she adored Dora's sensual massages, sometimes she could use something a little more therapeutic. Jessica enrolled Zachary in the course and sent the schedule and class information to his e-mail. She sighed, knowing he probably also needed more physical affection. Although she preferred sex with Dora, Jessica could make an effort to to hug him more often. At least a little went a long way with Zachary and he seemed to appreciate any attention.

She shut down the laptop and handed it to Zachary to return to her office. When he came back to the living room, she patted the sofa besides her. He looked at her with his head tilted to one side and his eyebrows drawn together, but didn't move. She patted it again and he slowly crawled to the sofa. She grabbed his hair and pulled until he climbed up next to her. Jessica pushed his head toward her thigh and he smiled. Taking a deep breath he curled up on his side with his head in her lap. She stroked his hair and the boy made a noise in his throat that almost sounded like a cat's purr.

Z

Although he enjoyed taking care of Mistress' house, Zachary relished the opportunities to serve her in more personal ways. When he pleased her most, she allowed him to massage her whole body -- a privilege usually only awarded to Miss Dora. Zachary cherished those moments, even though they inevitably caused him great pain. In his course work, the instructors lectured about never having sexual thoughts or interactions with a client. But Mistress wasn't a client.

Summoned to her room the first time after he received his certificate from the online school, Zachary found Mistress waiting for him, laying face down on her bed. Just the sight of her smooth back, her rounded rear, her long, lovely legs, resulted in crushing pain as he swelled within the confines of his plastic cage. Zachary saw the bottle of massage oil on the nightstand. He poured some into his hands and rubbed his palms together to warm it, the way the school taught, and kneaded it into her shoulders, her back, her legs, Zachary so enjoyed the feel of Mistress' silky soft skin under his slick-with-massage-oil hands, the pain didn't trouble him.

The first time he touched her rear, his hand shook. He yielded to impulse and planted a kiss on each cheek. Fortunately, Mistress didn't seem displeased by this, so Zachary decided to incorporate that move into his repertoire. He knew the instructor wouldn't approve, but doubted he would have further contact with the woman.

When he finished her back and legs, Mistress turned over and allowed Zachary to rub oil into her beautiful breasts, her rounded belly, and the rest of her front. Then, much to his delight, Mistress opened her legs, releasing the musk smell that had gotten stronger as he massaged her, creeping out to tantalize him. She tasted so divine. She let him lick her and suck on her clit until she came and generated more luscious juices for him to imbibe.

By the time Mistress pushed his shoulders away with her heels, Zachary couldn't think because his groin hurt so badly. He feared he would pass out and was actually grateful that Mistress sent him back to the dungeon. As soon as he got downstairs, he stepped into the shower and turned on the cold water. That combined with concentrating his thoughts on the various items outside the bathroom that Mistress could use to hurt him, helped reduce the swelling and ease the pain.

Chapter Eight

When Miss Dora walked in through the door from the garage one Tuesday, even Zachary could see the exhaustion on her face. On Tuesdays, Miss Dora returned home before Mistress. Every other day of the week she worked at the bookstore until quite late and Zachary would reheat the dinner he had made for Mistress to serve Miss Dora when she finally arrived.

"You look very tired. Would you like me to give you a massage before Mistress gets home?" Zachary knelt on the wooden floor of the kitchen in front of the stove while Miss Dora removed her clothing and hung it on a hook by the door.

She stared at him. "I'm not sure Mistress would approve of that."

"Why? If I give you a massage, you'll have more energy to serve Mistress when she returns." Although Mistress referred to Miss Dora as his sister slave, Zachary tended to think of her more as his superior. She sat at the table with Mistress and shared Mistress' bed. She got to lick Mistress every night and Mistress allowed Miss Dora to bathe and dress her each morning.

Miss Dora pulled a bottle of Perrier mineral water out of the frig. "Look, Zachary, you're a nice boy, but..."

"I'm only going to rub your back. Not like when Mistress

allows me to massage her. I know you don't like men." Not that Zachary wouldn't have enjoyed touching Miss Dora all over the way Mistress permitted him to touch her. But he saw a need he could meet and his desire to serve in this house included Miss Dora as well as Mistress.

She smiled. "Sure, why not."

Zachary followed Miss Dora up to Mistress' bedroom enjoying the sight of her backside, much rounder and plumper than Mistress', in front of him. He wondered if Miss Dora wasn't a lesbian whether Mistress would have let him have sex with her. He had never had intercourse with a woman. He would have liked to experience that just once before Mistress locked him up.

He shrugged. Maybe that would have made the confinement worse. If he knew what it felt like, perhaps he would regret his chastity more. As it was, he missed the sensation of stroking himself with his hand. Once a week, Mistress milked him using a prostate massager. Although he enjoyed how the special dildo felt when she pushed it into him, he often longed for the release of ejaculation.

Miss Dora lay face down on the bed, and Zachary warmed the massage oil in his hands. Her skin felt as silky as Mistress', but her body had a softer feel. And Miss Dora had none of Mistress' lovely, musky smell. He could feel the tension in her muscles relax under his fingers and wondered what had caused her such stress. Normally, Miss Dora took everything in stride.

Zachary worked the muscles of Miss Dora's shoulders, neck, and back, careful not to touch her rear or let his fingers slide down and caress her breasts as he sometimes could do with Mistress. While he enjoyed stroking her skin, she didn't generate the pain in his groin that came from massaging Mistress.

When he stopped, Miss Dora rolled over on her back. "Thanks, boy. You'd better go get dinner started."

"I've got a roast and potatoes in the oven." He glanced at the clock on Mistress' nightstand. "I'd should go make the salad and set the table."

Z

Jessica watched Zachary eat his dinner out of the dog dish on the floor by the refrigerator. She had moved his food and water bowls upstairs so he could eat when she and Dora did. She often found it amazing how low she had taken the boy. Although she had used similar techniques to those employed by Professor Lawrence, when he broke her she had retained a sense of self. She had struggled against the submission he required and she had broken free despite his efforts to blackmail her. She still visited Tom and Roger each week and once a month mailed the professor a check. He had referred a dozen clients to her and she had dutifully paid him the agreed commission. But, except for the occasional faculty/student parties at the Professor's house, she never saw the man anymore.

Jessica took another bite of meat and resisted the urge to leave the table and go find her laptop. As fascinating as she found the psychology of slavery, she could never publish any research that delved deeper into the subject. Still, comparing the results of her breaking and Zachary's might help her find an alternative to drug therapy. The klonopin caused him amnesia and occasional hallucinations. But the other drugs she had tried had even worse side effects.

"Get me a pad of paper and a pen." Jessica didn't direct her command at either in particular, but Zachary bolted for the den before Dora could rise from her chair. In a moment he knelt in front of her, offering the requested items.

"Good boy." Jessica patted his head and took a sip of merlot before she scribbled some notes on the pad.

The Professor let her return home after he broke her. The servitude he required did not include living in his home and he only locked her up in chastity when he sent her to submit to his colleagues. Then, too, Zachary had multiple problems preventing him from enjoying life on his own. Except for money, she had never lacked the means to function independently.

She set down the pen. At least Zachary seemed to thrive in the strict environment she had created for him. The protocols and rituals she required helped him manage his anxiety. Although he still needed drugs, she had cut his klonopin dosage down to the minimum. Pain seemed to work for him as treatment for his depression. And with precise instructions on how to behave, his Aspergers didn't prevent him from functioning within the household.

Still, Jessica could not envision Zachary living on his own. Except when she took him to doctor and dentist appointments, the only time he had left her house during the past twenty months was for his tattoo.

The phone rang and Dora rose to get the handset before Zachary could lift his head from his supper bowl. Dora handed the phone to Jessica and she pressed the on button.

"Dr. Jessica Richards?" The male voice on the telephone exuded somber authority and the hairs on the back of Jessica's neck stood erect.

"Yes?" With Dora and Zachary both accounted for, she couldn't imagine who else authorities might contact her about.

"This is Sgt. Weston of the Highland Park Police. Do you know an Alyssa Volker?"

Jessica gasped in panic. "Is she hurt? Where is she?" She rose to her feet and put her hand over the speaker. "Get my shoes and coat," she told Dora.

"No, Mrs. Volker was not involved in the accident. But Mr. Volker was killed and I'm afraid Mrs. Volker is somewhat hysterical. She gave us your telephone number when we asked if there was someone she wanted us to call. Can you come to the Highland Park Hospital?"

"Tell her I'm on my way." Tears flooded Jessica's eyes and she blinked rapidly to clear her vision. Poor Alyssa. What would she do without Klark?

Dora slipped the shoes she had discarded when she entered her house only an hour ago onto her feet and held out her leather coat. "Do you wish me to go with you, Mistress."

Jessica grabbed her purse and headed for the garage. "No. And don't wait up. I don't know how late I'll be."

Her limited vision and the thought of how Alyssa would flounder without Klark to serve her, kept her from breaking half a dozen traffic laws on the way to Highland Park. She parked the Mustang in the first spot she found and stumbled into the Emergency Room. A woman in blue scrubs looked up when Jessica leaned on the desk.

"I'm here for Alyssa Volker." Those words sounded so wrong to Jessica's own ears. Alyssa had always been the strength Jessica leaned on: through her parents death, her financial troubles, her issues with the Professor. The woman gave Jessica a blank stare. "Is she a patient?" Jessica braced herself against the desk, trying to stop trembling. "I believe her husband, Klark, was brought here."

"I just came on. Let me check." The woman walked away from the desk.

Jessica saw a police officer talking to a nurse outside a doorway. "Excuse me, officer," she shouted. "Are you Sgt. Weston?"

The man looked up. "No, but I can get him for you."

Jessica shook her head. "I'm here for Alyssa Volker. Her husband ..." Jessica choked on the words.

The officer said something to the nurse, then walked over

to the glass doors separating the reception area from the rest of the Emergency Room. He held one door open. "Are you Dr. Richards?"

Jessica nodded and followed him past several empty wheelchairs and into the room where the nurse had gone. Equipment filled much of the available floor space. Klark lay on a gurney, the left side of his face smashed in, blood covering his mangled left arm and leg, and a tube sticking out of his throat. Alyssa, her hair flying in every direction, her coat stained with blood, clung to him, whispering "Don't you dare leave me, boy," over and over. Jessica suppressed a sob.

Another police officer stopped scribbling notes in a notebook and stepped over to Jessica. "Dr. Richards?"

She nodded, unable to speak.

"If you could get Mrs. Volker to release the body, we'd like to get it over to the coroner. We want to prosecute the guy who did this and the more evidence we have, the better our chances of putting him in jail."

Jessica touched Alyssa's arm and with great effort kept her voice calm. "He's gone, dear. You can't bring him back."

Alyssa shook her head so hard Jessica feared her neck would snap. Tears streaming down her face, Jessica wrapped her fingers around her friend's arm and pulled her away from the gurney. "You need to let the police do their job so they can arrest whoever did this." Jessica pulled Alyssa into her arms.

With a sob, Alyssa collapsed against Jessica, almost bringing her to her knees. Sgt. Weston helped Jessica lead Alyssa out of the room to a lounge area with a number of padded chairs. They sat her down in one of them, and Jessica took the seat next to her. Alyssa wept, her entire body shaking and her tears dampening Jessica's blouse. Jessica stroked Alyssa's hair and tried to think of comforting things to say. But the only thing that came to Jessica's mind was how devastated she would feel if something similar happened to Dora.

Chapter Nine

The metal chair pressed into the top of Alyssa's back, leaving her without the support she needed for the lower portion. Awareness of the pain penetrated the fog that had engulfed her brain, but didn't allow anything else in. The voice of the priestess standing by the mahogany casket drifted towards her, but the words didn't register. When friends got up to speak or to kneel before her and murmur their meaningless platitudes, she tried to grasp the size of the crowd that had turned out. But she couldn't differentiate the faces, the voices. Someone put a small packet of tissue in her hands, and she wondered why.

Alyssa allowed Jessica to pull her to her feet and she leaned on her with one arm while the other found its way to the small of her own back, rubbing at the sore muscles. Her back hadn't hurt this much since she first injured it nearly a decade ago and by then she had sent Klark to massage school. She gasped for breath, as the memories assaulted her of his strong hands on her back easing away the day's tensions. She just had to make it to the car, and Jessica would drive her home. Her feet sank into the wet grass and moisture penetrated her shoes.

Jessica adjusted her stance to take more of her weight and Alyssa realized if her friend let go she would collapse. One step at a time, she told herself. She looked up, but the car still seemed a mile away even though they left the gravesite ... Alyssa tried to grasp how long since she watched Klark's coffin lowered into the ground. She looked up at the bright clouds but couldn't see the sun to judge where it stood in the sky. Step, step, step. *Why didn't the car seem any closer?*

When they finally reached the blue Mustang, Jessica opened the passenger side door. Alyssa remembered that Klark would never hold a car door open for her again. She collapsed onto the seat bawling. Jessica lifted Alyssa's feet into the car and pulled the seatbelt around her before shutting the door.

Neither spoke during the drive back to Chicago. When Jessica pulled the car into the garage, another woman opened the door for Alyssa and she vaguely remembered that Dora had stood behind Jessica at the funeral, carried their purses to the car, and squeezed into the back seat behind Jessica before they drove away. With Dora on one side and Jessica on the other, Alyssa made it into the house, through the kitchen, and into the living room. They had just helped her to a couch so she could sit down when the doorbell rang.

Within moments, people filled the house. Someone brought her a plate of food. She wondered who had prepared it, but she couldn't imagine eating it. Dora pulled off her shoes and Alyssa curled her legs up on the sofa. People kept saying how sorry they were, what a tragic loss she had suffered. No one mentioned the piece of shit who got stinking drunk and plowed his SUV into her blue Toyota, totaling the car and destroying her life. Alyssa ignored all the people who had invaded her home and her grief, and turned her thoughts to how she would make that son of a bitch pay for what he had done to her.

Z

Alyssa stared at the basket full of folded laundry on top

of the dryer and again cursed the driver of the green Explorer. She hadn't done a load of laundry since acquiring Klark nearly two decades ago -- long before her back started giving her trouble. How would she carry the load up to her bedroom, today and every week from now on? She rubbed her knuckles into the small of her back, testing, relaxing, easing away the discomfort that had replaced the pain but that never quite disappeared except when Klark kneaded his magic fingers into her muscles.

With a hand on either side, she pulled the basket to her chest and turned toward the stairs. One at a time, careful to maintain her balance, aware of her posture, she ascended. At the top of the stairs, she assessed her distress level. Not bad. Not much worse than when she started. She set the laundry basket on the bureau and kneaded her back again with her fists. If she moved with care, if she stayed aware, she could cope. She dropped into the recliner and wept.

Z

Jessica waited outside Alyssa's brownstone. Since the funeral, Alyssa had refused to allow anyone in her house. Jessica had offered to send Dora or Zachary over to clean for her, but Alyssa declined each time. When she finally emerged from the house and locked the front door, Jessica was dismayed to see how old Alyssa looked now. She walked stooped over, moving slowly down the stairs and hesitating before she lowered herself into the Mustang's passenger seat.

"Where would you like to go for lunch?" Jessica depressed the clutch and eased the car into gear.

"Don't care really. Wherever you'd like." Alyssa pulled out the seatbelt and tucked in the buckle. She sat clutching her black leather shoulder bag in her lap.

"How bout Chop House, you like it there." Jessica mourned not only the loss of Klark, but the loss of her friend. She had finally persuaded Alyssa to accompany her to lunch, remembering how much that had helped when she lost her parents, but Alyssa had changed so much.

"Oh, that's much too fancy. And expensive. I don't have much money these days."

"I told you, this is my treat." After all the times Alyssa had taken her out to lunch when she barely had enough money for rent, Jessica enjoyed finding herself in a position to reciprocate. "Thanks to all the Professor's referrals, my practice brings in a nice income and I still get quite a bit from the two professor's I Domme."

"Don't know how you can do that, dear. I hated working as a pro."

Jessica hated the work also. Alyssa had nailed it when she said once that when they paid for her services the clients, not the Domme, had the control. But she didn't dare further antagonize Professor Lawrence by abandoning Tom and Roger. "Oh, it's not so bad. They're sweet boys and I enjoy the extra money. They pay well." Jessica turned and smiled at Alyssa, hoping to alleviate her concerns about where to eat lunch. "Would you prefer McCormick & Schmick's?"

"To be honest, dear, it's just nice to get out of the house for a change. Wherever you decide is fine with me."

The lack of emotion in her voice along with the extra lines that had appeared around her eyes made Jessica wince. She wondered if Alyssa had had as much trouble cheering her up after her parents' deaths. "You haven't replaced your car yet?"

"No reason to. I don't really want to drive."

"What have you been doing with yourself?" Jessica turned the car toward Lake Shore Drive and headed in the direction of the Loop, grateful to have Alyssa at least participate in the conversation.

"Oh, I've been keeping busy." Alyssa smiled for the first

time since she got in the car, but her grin sent a cold shiver down Jessica's back.

"Oh, really?"

"That schmuck who killed my Klark got off with a slap on the wrist."

Jessica worried about the turn the conversation was taking, but decided Alyssa probably needed to get her concerns out in the open. "Isn't the insurance company going after him?"

"Of course. And I've got a lawsuit filed against him, too. But that's only money and the guy has lots of that. That's how he got off so easily. His fancy lawyers paid off the judge, I'm sure. He's got four priors."

Jessica pulled the car into a garage and took the ticket from the machine to raise the gate. Once she parked, she walked around to help Alyssa out of the car. The woman almost pulled Jessica off balance, leaning on her arm all the way to the elevator. Jessica wondered if grief or pain slowed Alyssa's steps. She waited until the waiter seated them at an elegantly carved booth to ask.

"Are you in pain?" Jessica eyed the menu, but she knew what she wanted.

"My back hurts a lot. I'm not used to doing so much lifting and I miss Klark's massages." Alyssa's lips lifted, but the evil gleam still shone in her eyes. "I'm making that SOB pay for what he did to my Klark. I'm going to make him feel real pain."

Jessica's eyes opened wide. She leaned forward and whispered: "Surely you don't intend to ..."

Alyssa laughed. "No dear. Not that. I'm more creative. He's taken away Klark's life, so I'm taking away his, little by little. I stopped by his house periodically and picked up his mail until I got his bank and credit card statements. I used that information to close his checking and savings accounts. I had his utilities turned off, used his credit cards to spend a fortune on porn sites and had all kinds of smut delivered to his home. I've subscribed him to more than a hundred magazines and put him on the mailing list for every catalog that exists."

The waiter came over to take their order and, stunned by Alyssa's confession, Jessica forgot what she had planned to have. She had to send him away while she read the menu.

After he left, Alyssa continued. "I've applied for additional credit cards in his name so I've pretty well guaranteed he'll never get another card and I've maxed out all the ones he's got. After I subscribed his work e-mail address to a bunch of porn sites, I let his boss know, anonymously of course. He got fired last week." The glint in Alyssa's eyes got brighter. "I even managed to get a fake death certificate which I've sent to the unemployment office and Social Security. Of course that will also show up if anyone does a credit check which most employers do these days."

Jessica took a deep breath while the waiter showed her a wine bottle, opened it, and poured pinot gris into their glasses. She couldn't remember ordering anything to drink. "Alyssa, don't you think you've become somewhat obsessed with hurting this guy?" Jessica ignored Alyssa's raised glass and left hers sitting on the table. "Do you spend all your time on the Internet looking for new ways to make this man miserable?"

Alyssa shrugged. "Pretty much. But, what else have I got to do? I got so far behind in my classes after the accident, I had to drop out of this semester entirely. Fortunately, I had purchased an adequate life insurance policy on Klark so I won't have to go to work for a while, at least until I finish school. But, if the court's won't make that man pay for what he did to me, I will. He took away my Klark."

"It sounds like you've already ruined his life." Jessica tried to remain calm in the face of Alyssa's vitriol. "You've surely made it impossible for him to pay any kind of settlement." Jessica took a sip of the wine, but she really didn't taste it.

"He still has a house and a car and a boat." Alyssa lifted her glass and took another long sip.

Chapter Ten

After dropping Alyssa off at her house, Jessica tried to process all of her reactions to what her friend had told her and figure out what made her grip the steering wheel so tightly. She set aside how much Alyssa had changed and the horror of her persecution of the SUV driver. If that helped Alyssa cope with her grief and anger at losing Klark, Jessica couldn't really fault her. Although her methods weren't the exactly ethical, the guy deserved whatever Alyssa could do to him.

Lunch had gone later than Jessica had planned and now she found herself stuck in rush hour traffic. After sitting through three light changes while barely inching forward, she decided to forgo returning to the office. She had no appointments scheduled and had only planned on tackling insurance paperwork, anyway. When she finally got to the intersection, she turned right instead of going straight, heading home. Some jerk in a red sports car edged into traffic from a parking lot giving Jessica the choice of slamming on her brakes or hitting his car. The close call made her wonder again how she would react if Dora died in an automobile accident.

She honked at the sports car, and he had the audacity to wave. Jessica's grip on the steering wheel tightened until her knuckles turned white. She needed to stop comparing herself to Alyssa and wondering what her life would be like without Dora. Unlike Alyssa, Jessica had her career. If anything happened to Dora, she could at least console herself with her work instead of spending all her time online haunting a drunk driver.

Jessica clenched her teeth and the tension in her shoulders made her release the wheel with one hand and rub the back of her neck. Truth be told, except for the substantial income, she didn't enjoy anything about her practice. So many of her patients would never get better, at best she could only help them cope. Even though Zachary had improved immensely in the structured environment she had created for him, she saw no way to apply what she had done for him to anyone else.

Someone behind her leaned on his horn and Jessica realized the light had turned green. She moved forward through the intersection and thought of all the benefits of leaving the Chicago area. She lifted her briefcase from the back and set it on the passenger seat. Clicking it open with one hand while keeping the other on the wheel, she pulled out a yellow legal pad and propped it up on the steering wheel. May as well put the time stuck in traffic to good use.

Professor Lawrence appeared first on her list of reasons to leave. As long as she stayed in the Chicago area, she would never get completely free of him or his colleagues. Each time she returned home from a Dominatrix session with Tom or Roger, she felt dirty and often showered for half an hour or longer. Dora submitted to her out of love. Jessica adored the girl and couldn't imagine her life without her. Even Zachary's submission engendered affection for the boy -- feelings she never had for Tom or Roger -- although his dependence on her grated. She could never care for him the way she loved Dora.

The cars in front of her inched forward and Jessica's foot cramped from keeping it on the clutch. Add traffic to her list of reasons to move on. In fact, although she considered all her alternatives during the rest of the drive home, the right side of the pad stayed blank. Jessica couldn't think of one reason to stay in the area after Dora graduated next month. She almost wrote Alyssa's name on that side, but the woman had become a hermit obsessed with avenging herself on Klark's killer and Jessica questioned whether their relationship could continue.

Jessica needed to find a position that would let her do the kind of research she had given up to sign on with Professor Lawrence, preferably one that would pay a reasonable salary.

Z

"You cannot abandon that boy. You already violated every ethical canon in the book when you enslaved him without his consent." Alyssa tightened her grip on the phone.

"He consented. And, I'm sure he'll manage fine on his own." Jessica's nonchalance made Alyssa cringe.

"You really don't know that. The boy couldn't function on his own when you took him in, or at least that's the excuse you gave for enslaving him without consent." Alyssa tried to reign in her anger. She had known Jessica for nearly eight years and didn't want her running off to England with bad blood between them, especially after all the help Jessica had given her since Klark's death.

"A patient cannot consent to enslavement by his therapist any more than a child can consent to enslavement by his parent." Alyssa continued the argument, she couldn't back down if only for Zachary's sake. "Now, this boy's grown dependent on you. You've trained him to serve, to meet your needs at the expense of his own. How will he take care of himself? He hasn't held a job in more than two years. When was the last time he left the house? Will he know how to pay his own bills? How to shop for groceries? Can he even maneuver in the vanilla world any more? Have you really considered the consequences for him?"

"I don't have any choice." Jessica almost sounded as if she regretted releasing Zachary, and Alyssa wondered if she could get her to change her mind. "I can't get emigration papers for two partners, I'm having enough trouble getting a visa for a female Significant Other. Dora's my love I won't give her up. I only took Zachary in because he needed the pain and the structure."

"And why do you believe he needs that any less now? You broke him." Those words left a sour taste in Alyssa's mouth. Klark gave himself to her freely out of love and she cherished everything he did for her. She had never treated him like a feral animal. "You can't just throw him out and expect him to make his way in the vanilla world without retraining. Would you put a domesticated dog or cat out on the street without finding a new home for it?"

"Kind of hard to find a new home for a slave." Any regret had disappeared and Jessica's voice could have frozen water. "Why don't I give him to you? I know he's not going to take Klark's place, but I've trained him well. He could meet your needs. At the very least he could take over the housework and cooking. And he gives very nice massages."

The idea made Alyssa want to retch. She thought about how difficult managing without a slave had become. She'd hired a cleaning service, but she couldn't bear to let anyone else do her laundry or cook her food. She missed Klark so much, but not because she had no one to do her chores. She clutched her stomach. Having another boy around would create too much pain. "I'm sorry," she whispered. "I can't, it's too soon." Alyssa took a deep breath. "You need to find him another Mistress."

"Don't have time. I've got to dismantle the dungeon, get the house on the market. Plus closing my practice." Jessica sighed. "And, you wouldn't believe the tons of paperwork."

"You owe that boy more consideration." Alyssa's knuckles turned white as her grip on the phone tightened again. "You never got informed consent for what you did to him. And now, he's served you well for two years. You're responsible for that boy, collared or not, until you find him a new owner."

"Unless you take him, I'm afraid he'll have to manage on his own. Even if I stayed, I don't know that I could continue to take care of him. Gotta go. Lots to do." Jessica ended the call.

Z

Mistress ushered Zachary and Miss Dora into the living room. Miss Dora had spent the morning helping Zachary fold his jeans and tee shirts and place them in a canvass duffle bag along with a few of his favorite books and the MP3 player Mistress had bought him for Christmas. Boxes piled against the wall framed the window and the furniture all had little tags on it.

"Zachary, you have served me well over the past couple of years. I want you to know that my releasing you today has nothing to do with the quality of your work. But, I'm moving to London and I can't take you with me.

"Yes, Mistress. Thank you, Mistress." Zachary knelt on the floor in front of her confused by her words. Why couldn't he go with Mistress to Connecticut? Where would he live if she left him behind?

"When I placed this collar on you," Mistress touched

the links of the chain around his neck, "I told you no one could ever remove it except me." Mistress had a pair of pliers in each hand. She grabbed one of the links, with the pliers, pulled it open, and removed the chain from around his neck. "Hold out your hand, boy." Mistress voice had a slight hitch in it and Zachary worried she might be catching a cold.

Mistress let the links slide through her fingers onto his palm. "You may keep this, if you wish, to remember me by. If you'd like, when you find a new Mistress, you may give it to her to collar you with." Mistress dropped the open link on top of the others. "Stand up."

Zachary stood and Mistress unlocked the tiny padlock from the pin that attached the plastic cage encasing his penis to the ring around his balls. He remained standing, his hands behind his back, so Mistress could inspect his skin as she did about once a month or so. But she didn't remove the plastic pieces. Instead, she slipped the key ring over the hasp of the lock and closed it.

She pulled on his arm until he brought the hand holding the chain around to his chest and dropped the padlock and the key on top. "You may keep the CB or leave it here. But, I no longer hold your key. Now, go put your clothes on and I'll take you to your new home." Mistress reached up and stroked his hair and Zachary leaned against her hand until she pulled it away.

He backed away until he passed through the door to the living room, then turned and headed down the stairs. He waited until he reached the basement before removing the CB cage. For the first time in two years, he touched his own penis and closed his eyes when it sprang to attention. Mistress had told him to get dressed. But he needed to feel the soft skin under his fingers, needed to stroke it until he spurted.

Zachary heard footsteps on the stairs. He stepped into the bathroom where Miss Dora had left a pair of jeans, white cotton briefs, and a red tee shirt that said "Give Peace a Chance" in white letters on the toilet seat. He unhinged the ring around his ball sack and placed it with the pins, the cage, and the metal chain on top of the clothing in his duffle bag. He added the padlock, the closing link, and the key and zipped the bag shut. Carefully, he set the pile of clothing on top of the duffle, lifted the toilet seat and lid, and stood in position.

He missed the toilet the first try, spraying the rim and wetting the floor. Mortified, he ran to get some paper towels to clean up the mess.

Miss Dora stood by the stairs. "It's okay, boy. You probably just need to practice once or twice to get used to doing it that way, again. Don't worry about it."

When he had cleaned up the mess and washed his hands, Zachary slipped into the clothing. The cloth felt soft against his erection and he had to adjust himself to get his jeans zipped up.

When he followed Mistress toward the garage, Zachary noticed Miss Dora still had no clothes on. He turned to her.

"Guess this is goodbye, Zachary." Miss Dora put her arms around his waist and squeezed him against her wonderful full breasts.

Zachary stood with his hands at his side, wanting more than anything else to lean down and kiss Miss Dora, but not knowing what to do. For the past two years she had treated him like a brother, laughing with him when Mistress went to conferences, allowing him to massage her almost every week, letting him tell her about what he learned from reading Nietzsche even though he knew she disagreed with his philosophy. Now she acted as if he would never see her again.

Miss Dora put one hand on each cheek to pull his face down toward her, stood on tiptoe, and planted a kiss on Zachary's forehead. "You take care of yourself, boy."

Zachary felt wet on his cheeks and wiped the back of his

hand across it. He realized he was crying and tried to remember the last time he had done that.

"Come on, boy." Mistress reached for the knob on the door to the garage and Zachary rushed to open it for her. He followed her out to the car and held her door until she had seated herself and put on her seatbelt. Closing the door, he started to walk toward the passenger .

Mistress rolled down her window. "Your duffle, boy, don't forget your duffle."

Zachary went back to the house and Miss Dora handed him the bag. Mistress popped the trunk and he placed it in there and pushed down the lid. The minute he closed the passenger side door, Mistress backed out of the garage.

"I've found a group of students who will let you stay with them for a few weeks in exchange for doing housework and fixing up the place. But then you'll need to get a job and pay your share of the rent or find a room for yourself somewhere." Mistress watched traffic and didn't look at him. "You remember the paper you signed before I brought you home, when I released you from treatment at the clinic?"

Zachary didn't know what she meant, but he nodded his head.

"You promised you would never tell anyone about the treatment I gave you at my house. That means you can never let anyone know that you served as my slave or any of the things that you did in my home." They sat at a red light and Mistress turned and looked straight at him. "Do you understand what I'm saying?"

Zachary lowered his eyes. "Yes, Mistress. Thank you, Mistress."

Chapter Eleven

Zachary worked in the music store for a week, at the bookstore for day and a half, and at the convenience store for three hours. Everywhere he applied after that looked at his application and told him they had already offered the job to someone else or they were reconsidering whether they wanted to fill the position.

On the one hand, he enjoyed the freedom of wandering around outside whenever he wished. On the other, he missed knowing what to do with his days. He kept the house where he lived immaculate, did everyone's laundry, and if they gave him money for food he cooked dinner for them. He pulled up the old carpeting in the living room that smelled of piss and stale beer and replaced it with a perfectly good piece he found leaning up against a garbage can down the street. His roommates asked him to move out after six weeks.

Desperate, Zachary called his mother for the first time in almost three years.

"My god, Zachary, where have you been? I've been worried sick about you, expecting to get a call from the cops any day telling me they had found your body." He thought he heard a sob at the other end of the line.

"I had some trouble with my depression." Zachary paused and took a deep breath. He had no idea how to explain the past two years to his mother, wasn't sure he wanted to, and thought Mistress probably wouldn't appreciate it if he did. "I was in an experimental treatment program for a while, but the funding ran out. I haven't been able to find a job and I don't have anywhere to stay."

"Where are you?"

"Chicago."

"Can you get to the train station downtown?"

Zachary wondered if one of his former roommates would drive him. He stuck his hands in his pockets and came up with a dollar ninety- five in change. Not enough for the bus. "I'll manage."

"I'll pay for a ticket and you can pick it up at the station. How soon can you get there?"

"Better make it tomorrow."

Z

His mom got Zachary a job at the loading dock where she worked. She let him stay in her basement and he had his own room and bathroom and a small refrigerator and hot-plate if he wanted to cook for himself. He didn't like the man his mother had married, part of why he had left Milwaukee in the first place. So Zachary spent most of his time alone in his room. He used his first paycheck to buy a computer.

As soon as the cable installer left, Zachary logged onto the Internet. Hands shaking, he typed in the URL of a website he remembered stumbling across when he searched for slave protocols online at Mistress' home. Then, he hadn't dared stay on the site once he saw what it involved. Now he sought it out eagerly. The site charged a fee, but the pictures used to entice men to give their credit card information served Zachary's needs. Looking at FemDoms dressed in leather with thigh-high, spike-heeled boots and gloves above their elbows, Zachary unzipped his jeans. Now that Mistress had unlocked him, he masturbated every night, sometimes two or three times.

When he finished, he surfed for a while, looking at BDSM personal sites and reading the profiles wishing he could find a Mistress to serve. He searched for information about Dr. Richards and ran across an old press release from when she opened her practice. Staring at her face, he remembered how wonderful she tasted, how soft her skin felt under his hands. He had gotten hard again and stroked himself while thinking about the delicious rounded mounds of her breasts.

Zachary stopped before he came. Somehow it didn't seem right to have an orgasm while staring at the woman who had locked him up for two years. He imagined she wouldn't appreciate that. But, looking at her face while he touched himself brought her closer, made it easier to remember how much he enjoyed serving her. He bookmarked the page.

The job on the loading dock lasted six weeks. When he got fired, Zachary decided his mother could support him. She owed him. After all, she had sent him to stay with his uncle when his father left. Sometimes he thought about telling her, now that he remembered, what had happened that year. But every time he tried to broach the subject, his anger at her for allowing the abuse flared up and he just sputtered. He wondered if he should ask Dr. Johansson about confronting her.

Tall and stocky, Dr. Nathan Johansson had hair and beard the color of used steel wool. He made Zachary lie on a couch during their sessions and talk into a tape recorder. He always wore grey or navy pinstripe suits and had a pipe in his hand or his teeth. Zachary had never seen him smoke it, but the man reeked of apple-flavored tobacco which made Zachary nauseous.

"Mr. Smith, I can't be of any help to you if you refuse to explain what sort of treatment you received under your previous therapist."

"Experimental." Zachary had promised Mistress he wouldn't tell anyone about her treatment and he wished Dr. Johansson would stop asking.

"That's not very informative, Mr. Smith. I'm not sure why you're so reticent. I've probably read about any therapy Dr. Richards might have tried."

Zachary shook his head. He couldn't understand why Dr. Johansson kept insisting that he share this information. "I signed a confidentiality agreement."

"Well, anything you tell me is protected under doctor-patient privilege so explaining your therapy would not violate your confidentiality agreement."

Zachary took a deep breath. If Dr. Johansson couldn't tell anyone what he said, then Mistress couldn't get upset with him for talking about her treatment. And maybe if Dr. Johansson understood how much Mistress had helped Zachary, the psychiatrist could assist him in finding a new owner. "She kept me in her dungeon as her slave."

He heard Dr. Johansson's pipe drop on the floor. The therapist leaned over and picked it up. "And what did being Dr. Richards' slave entail, Mr. Smith?"

"She beat me when I had depressive episodes. The first time it took a lot to bring me out of it. But after that, she usually only had to flog me once or twice a month or so. I learned to enjoy the pain. It's kinda like getting drunk."

Dr. Johansson shifted in his seat. "What else?"

"I never wore clothing in the house. And she kept me locked up in chastity."

"Chastity?"

Suddenly Zachary felt his face grow hot and the thought of explaining to this man he had known only a few weeks about living locked in a plastic cage made him want to run from the room. "That's not really important. I cleaned her house, cooked food for her and her other slave ..."

"She had more than one slave?"

"Yes. Although I think you could say Miss Dora was more of her lover than her slave, she still couldn't wear clothing in the house, called her Mistress, and always knelt before her."

"I see." Dr. Johansson swallowed audibly. "Tell me more about your enslavement."

"Mistress sent me to an online school so I could learn how to give her massages." Zachary smiled at the memory of Mistress' sweet taste. "I liked it when she allowed me to touch her."

"Did she abuse you sexually as well?"

"Oh, no. Mistress never abused me." Zachary frowned. He had told Dr. Johansson about his childhood; the man should understand the difference. "She only beat me to prevent another severe depressive episode. When I pleased her, she let me massage her and lick her." Zachary ran his tongue over his lips. "When she didn't need me, a lot of time she let me read or research things on the Internet."

"What kind of things did you research?"

"I learned more about the lifestyle, about protocols and rituals." Zachary missed the rituals. They gave meaning to his day-to-day existence and prevented the anxiety attacks he had regularly since Mistress sent him away.

"Lifestyle?"

"That's the term people use who live in Dominant/submissive relationships." Zachary stopped himself from saying D/s. Somehow, he knew Dr. Johansson wouldn't understand the acronym. He probably couldn't help Zachary find a new owner, either.

"And why do you call this an experimental treatment? It

seems the only benefit for you was the beatings to interrupt your depressive cycles. You probably would have been better off with drug therapy."

"Oh, no." Zachary sat up and swung his legs over the couch. "I loved everything about serving as Mistress' slave. Her rituals helped keep me from having anxiety attacks. I still took klonopin, but not nearly as much as I need now. I had things to do with my days that meant something to someone. Mistress always told me what a good boy I was." Zachary had to press his lips together to stop the trembling before he could continue. He missed Mistress and Miss Dora so much.

"She would pet me all the time and every once in a while she would hug me. While she read or watched television she would pat the sofa and let me crawl up and put my head in her lap. I never had to worry about what other people thought, or if I was saying something wrong, or how people might react to what I did. In Mistress' house, I always knew my place, knew what to do. She made sure I had enough to eat, that I didn't sleep too much, that I took a shower every day."

"You realize, Mr. Smith, that not only was Dr. Richards' behavior highly unethical, it probably was illegal as well. It appears she brainwashed you into believing that serving as her indentured servant benefitted you in some way."

"But it did." Zachary realized he had made a horrible mistake confiding in Dr. Johansson. He had to convince the man how much he had benefitted from Mistress' treatment. "Before Mistress brought me home, I'd lost my job, I was going to get evicted from my room, I'd lost twenty pounds, and I slept most of the time. I did nothing productive."

Dr. Johansson tapped his pipe against his lips. "Wasn't this particular depressive episode brought on by Dr. Richards' insistence that you remember the sexual abuse you allegedly suffered as a child?"

"That's not the point." Dr. Johansson made it sound as if Mistress was to blame for Zachary's depression.

"Actually, Mr. Smith, it may very well be the point." Dr. Johansson looked at his watch. "I'm afraid your time is up today. We'll continue this on Thursday and we can discuss your options regarding Dr. Richards' abuse."

Zachary stomped out of the office and down the stairs to the small lobby on the main floor. Dr. Richards never made him leave if his session ended in the middle of something important. He debated not returning to see Dr. Johansson again. His klonopin and paroxetine prescriptions would last for two more months. Surely he could find a new therapist by then. But what if he didn't come back and Dr. Johansson tried to get Dr. Richards in trouble? Zachary chewed on his lip while he waited at the bus stop, sweat dampening his shirt and the sun burning his skin.

Chapter Twelve

Alyssa read the e-mail three times, growing more disgusted with each reading. Jessica expected her to go find out what had become of Zachary. How could a woman she thought was her friend impose on her that way?

"Dearest Alyssa," Jessica wrote. "Getting settled in took longer than I expected. You would not believe how much paperwork I had to complete so dora could look for a job. she still hasn't found one, but she's had some freelance assignments referred through the University and a few folks she knows in the States. W/we've found a lovely flat near the West End. No room for a dungeon, but there's clubs W/we can go to when we want to play."

Alyssa had so enjoyed taking Klark to clubs and Lady Gina's parties. With his body still muscular despite his age, he always made her proud that he wore her collar. He behaved so much better and could take so much more pain than most of the other boys. Jessica's e-mail just reminded her how much she missed her slave.

"I was wondering if you could be a dear and check up on Zachary. I haven't heard from him since I left Chicago. I've tried to call his cell, but the number's disconnected and e-mail just bounces back."

Although a nice boy, Zachary was not her responsibility and Alyssa resented Jessica's request.

"I'm afraid I don't have time to look after your slave," Alyssa wrote in response. "You should have found him a new owner instead of releasing him." She logged out of her e-mail, turned off her computer, and curled up in the corner of the sofa. Daylight faded to dusk, but Alyssa didn't turn on any lights. She just let the links of the chain that used to hang around Klark's neck flow from one hand to the other.

Z

"Mr. Smith, after a great deal of thought, I have a course of action to recommend to you." Dr. Johansson flipped through the typed pages in a file folder.

For once, Dr. Johansson let Zachary sit in a chair across from his desk while he spoke. That alone made Zachary nervous and he had to sit on his hands.

"I am very concerned about your obsession with finding someone to own you." Dr. Johansson curled two fingers of each hand around in a quotation mark movement. "I think between your depression, anxiety, masochism, and social inadequacies, you probably would function better in a controlled environment."

"But that's exactly why I want to find an owner." Zachary had spent weeks online, responding to advertisements, answering questions, and trying to politely inquire about the preferences of those with whom he had communicated. He couldn't even find anyone interested in trying him out.

"That is not what I had in mind. What you experienced with Dr. Richards was an abusive situation from which you've failed to recover. It certainly would not be appropriate for me to allow you to seek out another such abusive situation." Dr. Johansson closed the file and folded his hands together on top of it. "No, I think commitment to an institution offers the safest environment for someone with as many problems as you have, especially given your inability to hold a job or maintain a place to live on your own."

Zachary picked his feet up off the floor and hugged his knees to his chest. He didn't understand why Dr. Johansson thought an institution could be a safe place. But, no one wanted him. That he understood. Mistress had removed his collar and left the country. His roommates had kicked him out. His mother's husband constantly complained about how much he ate and the electricity he used for his computer.

"In an institutional environment, you would receive the care you need and no one would abuse you."

Zachary shrugged.

Z

After half a dozen pleading e-mails from Jessica, Alyssa decided she could at least visit the house where Jessica had made arrangements for Zachary to stay. Jessica had helped her survive those first few months without Klark. With the taxi waiting in the driveway, she climbed up the wooden steps to the front porch. Looking through the window, she saw several students sprawled across various pieces of furniture. A youngster with sandy blond hair and a huge stud in his nose answered the door.

"I'm looking for Zachary Smith. He moved in here about five months ago."

The boy turned to a girl with purple hair who wore a black body stocking and lay on her stomach across a large red bean bag. "Til, you know bout a Zachary Smith?"

She looked up from a book that probably weighed five pounds. "He only lasted like a month or something. Weird dude."

Alyssa stifled her reaction to that comment coming from a woman who had a dozen rings in each ear, one above her eyebrow, and another through her upper lip. "Do you know where he went?"

"Jeb, didn't Zach say something about his mom up in Milwaukee?"

An impossibly skinny boy unwound his six-foot-three frame from where he had curled up in the corner. He shuffled through a doorway at the far end of the room and ten minutes later returned with a scrap of pink paper in his fingers. "Don't know where he went." He handed the paper to Alyssa. "E-mail."

"Thanks, thanks a lot." Alyssa looked at the scribbles.

The front door closed and the tall boy wandered back to his corner. Alyssa stuffed the paper in her pocket and hurried back to the air-conditioned comfort of the cab.

Z

When she next logged on, Alyssa composed an e-mail to Jessica to give her Zachary's e-mail address. She hesitated, cursor floating above the send button. Her friendship with Jessica began because she sensed the girl's detachment when they first took a class together shortly after Jessica's mother died. Alyssa had felt sorry for her and then when her father died a year later, Alyssa adopted Jessica, determined not to leave the girl adrift without her parents. Although Jessica had stepped up when Klark died, Alyssa still had so many misgivings about the woman over her treatment of Zachary. Alyssa decided she had no reason to continue her friendship with Jessica.

After pasting Zachary's address into a new e-mail, Alyssa deleted the one she had written to Jessica. Alyssa sent the boy a short note inquiring as to his well being. She did not mention Jessica's concern and had forgotten about him by the time she heard back three days later.

"Dear Lady Alyssa," he wrote. "i'm so honored that you have taken the time to inquire about me. Please be assured that arrangements are being made for my care. i disclosed the nature of my relationship with my former Mistress to the therapist that i currently am seeing including the circumstances surrounding my enslavement. i also have expressed my desire to be collared again, which this therapist stands adamantly against.

"my therapist has suggested i consider taking legal action against my former Mistress for engaging in unprofessional conduct, which i refuse to consider since i feel more good than harm came from the relationship. As a result of my quite unsuccessful attempts to find a new Owner, this therapist is working to have me declared mentally disabled so he can have me committed to an institution where he assures me i will receive the care i need."

Alyssa sat staring at the screen. What the hell did Jessica do to this boy?

Chapter Thirteen

After numerous e-mails and several phone calls, Alyssa finally persuaded Zachary to ask his therapist to put the commitment process on hold so he could come and visit her. He reported that his stepfather, grateful to get him out of the house, paid for the train ticket and a cab from the Glenview station to Alyssa's house.

When he rang her bell, Alyssa almost didn't recognize the boy. He had lost weight and shaved off his hair. His entire face drooped. She remembered the adoration the boy had shown Jessica and wondered for a moment if he might take Klark's place in her house.

She let him in and he dropped to his knees, covering her fuzzy slippers with kisses. "Thank you so very much, Lady Alyssa, for allowing me to serve you. I so very much miss serving and I have so longed to be at the feet of a Goddess again."

Alyssa had to lean against the door for support. Memories of Klark on his knees, his lips on her feet, brought tears to her eyes and a weakness to her knees. "You're still clothed boy, you know better." Alyssa walked away and dabbed the corner of her shirt sleeve against her eyes. She didn't want the boy to think he had upset her.

After he had made her dinner and cleaned up the kitchen, Alyssa sat on the couch and allowed the boy to massage her feet. Thoughts of Klark in that position made her stomach want to give up the tasty chicken Zachary had prepared for her. To drive the thoughts away, she asked him questions.

"What makes your current therapist believe you should take legal action against Lady Jessica?"

Zachary rubbed the heel of Alyssa's left foot with his thumbs. "He thinks she took advantage of her position as my therapist to enslave me and that she never obtained my consent."

"Did she?"

Zachary wrinkled his nose, but kept rubbing her foot. "Well, I signed a paper promising to never talk about how she treated my depression. And the first time she beat me, I agreed to try pain therapy." His thumbs moved up to Alyssa's arch. "But, I don't remember her asking me if I wanted to serve as her slave. I wasn't doing too well back then, so I'm not saying she didn't. I just don't remember."

Alyssa sighed. She hadn't had her feet worshiped in such a very, very long time. But his words prevented her from enjoying his efforts. She pulled her foot from his hands. "Exactly how did your enslavement come about, Zachary?"

He sat back on his heels and put his hands on his thighs, palms up. "Mistress took me to her home because I was sleeping all the time, I'd lost weight, I didn't bathe, I'd gotten fired from my job, and my landlord had started eviction proceedings."

"What caused such a deep depression?" Alyssa stuck her foot back out. No reason not to let him continue while he talked.

Zachary kissed her toes then resumed working her muscles with his thumbs. "Mistress got me to remember the sexual abuse I'd suffered as a child." His voice took on an atonal quality and his facial muscles tightened. "That triggered the most severe depressive episode I'd ever experienced. Mistress tried a bunch of different pills, most of which made me sick and none of which worked. Then she offered to treat me with pain. She explained that would release endorphins. I figured I didn't have anything to lose. After she beat me, she let me lick her and then locked me up in a cage." His face brightened and he almost smiled. "I don't remember exactly what happened next, but I think I went several days without sleep while Mistress and Miss Dora applied more pain. Then Mistress locked me in chastity and Miss Dora taught me how to serve her and Mistress sent me to an online massage school."

Alyssa couldn't move. She no longer felt Zachary's thumbs against the bottom of her foot. After several moments, she recovered from her shock enough to speak. "Do you understand that Lady Jessica should have explained all the repercussions of slavery and allowed you to choose whether or not you wanted to give yourself to her?" She remembered Zachary's collaring ceremony -- how one-sided it felt. At the time she had attributed that to Jessica's newness, or Zachary's shyness. Now, she understood.

"I do now." Zachary kissed her toes and switched to her right foot. "I've read a lot on the Internet since Mistress collared me."

"And now how do you feel about what happened?"

"If Mistress hadn't taken me in, I would have had no place to live, no job, and no will to survive. I probably wouldn't even still be around."

Alyssa sighed. "But, now that she's abandoned you, you're no better off than when she took you in. You still have no place to live, no job and your therapist wants to have you committed to an institution."

Zachary shrugged without taking his thumbs away from her feet. "Before she brought me home, I seriously thought about just letting myself starve to death. I enjoyed serving Mistress." He smiled. "I had two very wonderful years at her feet. And, I understand now that the British authorities would only allow her to take Miss Dora with her. If I could find another owner, I probably would do just as well as I did in Mistress' home. But, no one seems to want me. I'm damaged goods. So at least in an institution I'll have structure, someone to make sure I eat and take my meds." He shrugged without hesitating for a moment in his massage. "I forget sometimes."

Alyssa clenched her fists, her nails biting into the heels of her palms. If Jessica hadn't run away to England, Alyssa would go over to her house right now to demand she make amends for the abysmal, unethical, cruel, and most of all non-consensual way she had treated Zachary. A slave should always choose if, when, and who to give himself to. Not only had Jessica abused the doctor-patient relationship, she apparently had enslaved Zachary without any consent at all.

Alyssa made an effort to slow her breathing from the raging panting caused by her anger to a more normal in and out. Whatever had led to Zachary becoming a slave wouldn't change the reality of his situation. Jessica had broken him. He needed the D/s structure and environment to survive. Alyssa had to help him find it rather than allow his therapist in Milwaukee to lock the boy away in an institution.

Z

Zachary curled up in the metal cage that Alyssa had put him in for the night and took a long deep breath. Home. No, he couldn't describe the Domina who had locked the door of his cage as beautiful. Seeing her didn't excite him the way Lady Jessica had. But she had allowed him to cook for her and to worship her feet. She did have pretty feet with lovely soft skin. He had so missed the feel of a woman's skin under his hand. He thought about her insistence that he shouldn't move forward with the commitment proceedings, her conviction that he could find meaning in his life again.

Miss Dora had told Zachary about the accident that had taken the life of Lady Alyssa's slave. She had reported how devastated it left Lady Alyssa. He wondered if the Lady would allow him to stay and serve her. He adjusted the wool blanket Lady Alyssa had given him against the fall chill penetrating her basement so it covered his legs. He would most definitely prefer serving the Lady Alyssa to spending the rest of his life in an institution. He frowned. No, worshiping her feet hadn't turned him on. When Mistress had permitted him to do that, he swelled up inside the plastic cage. He smiled. If Lady Alyssa required him to serve in all the same ways that Mistress did, not getting turned on by her touch would prove less painful.

As much as he thought about the pros and cons, he really couldn't see a downside to wearing Lady Alyssa's collar. He just had to convince her that he could take care of her needs.

Chapter Fourteen

Alyssa watched Zachary in the laundry room, struggling to get the fitted sheets folded in a neat square. He put so much effort into minutiae, things she didn't care about. Some women wanted every item in their house placed in just the right way and micro-managed every little detail of service. Alyssa just wanted to know that the laundry would get washed, the house cleaned, and meals prepared. As long as she could find clean things when she needed them, she didn't care if the corners on the towels lined up perfectly.

She looked at the gleaming white washer and dryer, the dust- free shelf of canned goods, and the immaculate countertop and stepped into the room. Zachary dropped to his knees and leaned his head against her hip. He seemed to revel in any opportunity to glean affection from her.

When she stepped away, he returned to the pile of sheets.

"I appreciate having you around to do all the chores, boy." Of course, Zachary would never bring in the income that Klark had. "I don't enjoy having to take care of myself and I'm afraid I'm getting to old to keep up with everything around here."

"Thank you, Ma'am, but if I may say so, you're not that old."

Zachary smoothed the sheet he had folded and placed it in the laundry basket.

Alyssa wondered if she could ever grow as close to the boy as she had gotten to her pet. Klark had served as her slave, but he also was her lover, her friend, the joy of her life. Without him, living had lost its flavor. She sighed. "I'm older than I look, boy." Tears threatened to spill over her eyelashes and Alyssa turned away from the laundry room door to prevent Zachary from seeing. She couldn't expect the boy to take Klark's place. He would never fill the empty place in her heart, nor did she think she wanted him in her bed. That, he probably wouldn't want either, given the difference in their ages.

Zachary lifted the heavy laundry basket from the counter. "May I take these upstairs and put them away, Ma'am?"

Alyssa nodded. He did work very hard to please her. Surely she could find an arrangement that would meet both their needs. After all, every D/s relationship had its own unique dynamics. As Master Chris used to say: "Once you get past vanilla, you've got a myriad of flavors to choose from."

Z

When Alyssa gave Zachary permission to check the voice mail on his cell phone, he reported three messages from his mother and two from his therapist in Milwaukee. She listened while he told his mother he was enjoying his visit with his friend in Chicago and wasn't sure when he would return.

"You're angry with your mother, aren't you, boy?" she asked when he disconnected the call.

"She let it happen." His voice became flat.

It took a minute for Alyssa to realize what he meant. "Did she know about the abuse?"

Zachary shrugged. His facial muscles tightened.

"Who abused you, boy?" Alyssa softened her voice to a

whisper, concerned by Zachary's reaction to the mere mention of the incident.

"Uncle Paul." Zachary's atonal voice made Alyssa worry that he would slip into depression. But she could apply a whip as skillfully as Jessica, and she needed to understand his anger toward his mother.

"Your mother's brother or your father's."

"Father."

"Did you ever tell your mother what happened?"

Zachary turned his head slightly in either direction which Alyssa took as a no. She remembered reading, somewhere, about victims, especially children, blaming people who had no part in what happened rather than confronting their abuser.

"Then, how can you blame her?"

He pressed his lips together and stared at the floor. Alyssa sighed. She didn't have the training or knowledge to help him work it out and wondered if Jessica did either. She decided at this point changing the subject provided the safest option. "Why don't you return the call to your therapist."

"Yes, Ma'am." He dialed the number and left his information with whoever answered the call. When he disconnected, he set the phone on the floor in front of his knees and stared at it.

Alyssa laughed. "I don't imagine he'll call you back immediately. Give me the phone and I'll answer it. You may go start dinner."

"Yes, Ma'am. Thank you, Ma'am."

When Dr. Johansson called back, Alyssa told him to wait and put her thumb over the speaker on Zachary's cell. "Boy."

"Yes, Ma'am." He wiped his hands on a paper towel and knelt in front of her. She handed him the phone.

"Hello." He paused listening to the response.

"Yes, sir, I cancelled my appointments. I'm not living in Milwaukee at the moment." He sighed. "I'm staying with a

Lady who is a friend of my former Mistress."

Zachary's face got paler and sweat appeared on his lower lip. "I don't want to go into an institution." He gripped the phone tighter.

"I am hoping that this Lady will consider owning me, yes." He pressed his lips together. "I don't think you understand, sir ..."

His eyes darted back and forth.

Alyssa didn't like the turn the conversation appeared to take and held out a hand. Zachary handed her the phone and let out a long breath.

"Dr. Johansson?"

"Yes, who is this?" a deep male voice asked.

"The Lady Zachary spoke of." Something about the man's tone raised the hairs on the back of Alyssa's neck and made her feel very protective of the boy. "I just wanted to assure you that the boy is in good hands and whether or not I decide to accept ownership of him, I will make sure that he's well cared for."

"Slavery is illegal in this country, and I won't permit you to imprison my patient again."

Alyssa bristled at the tone of his voice. "Doctor, you have no call to speak to me in that manner. I have done nothing wrong and nothing illegal. I permit the boy to serve me, but I have not coerced him into doing so. He is free to leave at any time. He chooses to stay."

"Because you've brainwashed him," he sputtered.

Alyssa took a deep breath. Given what the man was told about how Jessica enslaved Zachary, she couldn't really blame him for his attitude. "While the methods used by the Lady Jessica could be considered brainwashing, I assure you that I do not employ them."

"Zachary needs the care he can only receive in an institution. He needs daily therapy and monitoring to make sure he takes his medication."

"What the boy needs is structure and an opportunity to serve. I have offered him both. In exchange I will take care of him, make sure he eats properly, and takes whatever medications he needs."

"I'll report you to the authorities."

For a moment, panic tightened Alyssa's chest. Then she smiled. "Fortunately, you don't know where I live, so you're going to find it difficult to do that." Alyssa pressed the button to end the call. She handed the phone to Zachary. "Turn this thing off."

"Yes, Ma'am. Thank you so very much, Ma'am."

Z

"Boy." Zachary loved it when Lady Alyssa called him that. It made him feel at home. He closed the dishwasher and hurried into the living room and assumed the position in front of the sofa where she sat with her legs curled up underneath her.

"Have you spoken with your therapist in Milwaukee since I hung up on him two weeks ago?"

He shook his head. "No, Ma'am. Except for that call, I haven't had any communication with him since I took the train down here." And Zachary hoped he would never have to speak with Dr. Johansson again. The man didn't understand his need to find an owner and Zachary much preferred serving over returning to institutional hell. "I never did tell him where I was going."

"Does he have any other way of reaching you?"

Zachary shook his head again. "I haven't checked my e-mail since I got here. I've kept my cell phone turned off and it probably needs charging anyway. I suppose he could call my mother, but she only knows I'm in Chicago."

"Have you thought about what you will do?" Lady Alyssa's voice took on a softer tone and Zachary wanted to rest his head in her lap like he used to do with Mistress. But Lady Alyssa only permitted him to touch her when she allowed him to worship her feet or give her a massage. She had never even let him lick her between her legs.

"I know what I would like to do." He kept his eyes pointed down, but tried to look up through his lashes to judge her reaction.

"And what is that?"

"I would like to serve you as your collared slave." He held his breath hoping she wouldn't become upset at his presumption.

"Why?"

Zachary looked up, puzzled, and quickly pointed his eyes down again. "Because I need to serve. I need the structure. I need to make a contribution. And, I would rather serve you than get locked up in the loony bin."

"But why me? Those are all reasons you wish to be collared by a Mistress. Why do you want to serve me? Why do you want to wear my collar?"

He tilted his head to one side. Strange questions. He thought about it for a few minutes before answering. "You've treated me kindly. You understand how to discipline and control a slave. You need a slave to take your pet's place." Zachary pursed his lips and brought his head upright. "And, I enjoy serving you. You make me feel wanted and secure."

Alyssa smiled. "You could probably find what you've described with a dozen or more Mistresses. But, I've enjoyed your service so far."

Zachary let out a sigh of relief.

"You work very hard to please. I'm not exactly sure whether this might work out long term given the difference in our ages. But I'm willing to put a training collar on you and give you the opportunity to earn a permanent one."

Confused, Zachary tilted his head to one side again. "A training collar?"

"Some people call it a collar of consideration. While you wear it, I treat you as my property and you accept me as your Mistress. But, I won't take complete ownership and responsibility for you and you can ask to leave at any time. If I decide to offer you my collar permanently, you then will have the opportunity to determine if that's the right choice for you." She put her feet, in her fuzzy purple slippers, on the floor. "What Jessica did to you was wrong in so many ways, on so very many levels. You should have had a chance to choose whether or not you wanted to give yourself to her. And, in reality, since she was your therapist, you were in no position to offer consent, even if she had given you that option. On this I agree with Dr. Johansson. You should take legal action against her."

Lady Alyssa rose to her feet. "But, one reality can't change and that is the fact that you are now a slave. I accept you into my service, and will consider you for my collar." She drooped a length of chain links around his neck and hooked the two ends together over the hasp of a small brass lock. This she clicked closed and pushed the numbers of the combination with her thumb to tumble them out of order.

"Thank you, Mistress." Zachary tried to understand the concept of earning Lady Alyssa's collar and deciding whether or not he wanted to wear it. His former Mistress had never given him that choice, nor had she ever expected him to prove himself worthy of her collar. She had trained him to meet her needs and disciplined him when he misbehaved. "May I ask a question?"

"Yes, boy." The Lady Alyssa, Mistress, still stood in front of him and he wished she would pat him on the head like Lady Jessica often did.

"What must I do to earn your collar, Mistress?"

She reached out her hand toward his cheek, but pulled back before she actually touched his skin. "Learn to serve me the way I wish to be served, not the way you served Lady Jessica. And understand, it's not just about how well you serve me. A D/s relationship requires chemistry and compatibility to work on all levels. That's not something you can create. It either develops or it doesn't. If it doesn't, you can't look at that as failure on your part."

"Yes, Mistress. Thank you, Mistress." He thought about Mistress Jessica's relationship with Miss Dora. He certainly had never enjoyed the level of chemistry and compatibility that those two had shared. He didn't think such a relationship possible with Mistress Alyssa, either. But he needed to serve.

"Did Lady Jessica require you to keep a journal?"

"Not really. But Miss Dora encouraged me to write my thoughts in a notebook. It did help keep me centered."

"I require that you keep a journal starting today. You can write in a notebook, or on the computer, I don't care. However, you must write in your journal every day. And you must make it available for me to read whenever I choose. I expect you to maintain scrupulous honesty in your journal. I will never discipline you for something I read in your journal, but you must never lie and I want you to record all your thoughts about slavery, serving me, and how you're feeling."

"Yes, Mistress. Thank you, Mistress." Zachary didn't believe he could reveal all his thoughts to Mistress Alyssa. How would she react to some of his more perverted fantasies?

"And, I'm not a psychologist." Her voice softened and again he longed for her to touch him. "You're going to have to let me know when you're getting depressed and need me to hurt you."

"Yes. Mistress. Thank you, Mistress." He hoped he could come to trust her that much.

Chapter Fifteen

Alyssa flipped through the pages of the red, spiral-bound notebook Zachary used as a journal. She couldn't understand half of what he wrote in it. He rambled on about Nietzsche, John Lennon, and metaphysical stuff that made no sense to a pragmatic. He referred to himself in the objective third person and he capitalized all pronouns referring to her or Jessica.

She perused the latest entry. "She not only listens to it," he had written, " but She genuinely understands it when it talks to Her in such a way that She can elaborate, crystallize, or otherwise complete its thoughts with something more poetically eloquent, insightful and profound. it is coming to cherish and revere the well of intellectual resources She has at her disposal. Her depth and education bemuses and inspires it and encourages it to be more candid when sharing its most personal thoughts; and in a way, having such an intellectually superior Counterpart is quite therapeutic."

Once more, as she had done countless time over the past few months, Alyssa cursed Jessica for enslaving him. The boy had a brilliant mind with the ability to understand complex philosophical subjects. True, he had dropped out of school before Jessica met him, but would he have returned to his studies if she hadn't enslaved him? Alyssa found she could discuss almost any topic with Zachary -- politics, music, movies, sociology, religion -- and discover new insights and awareness. Since her return to school, he had become quite useful because she could bounce ideas off him before outlining her term papers and research projects.

She closed the journal and rested her hands on top of it. She really couldn't claim the high road where Zachary was concerned. Like Jessica, she had essentially cut Zachary off from the external word. After repeated messages from Dr. Johansson that alternated between cajoling Zachary to return to therapy and threatening Alyssa with legal action, she had cancelled Zachary's cell service and closed his e-mail account. With a recommendation from Lady Gina, Alyssa had found Zachary a lifestyle-friendly therapist, but he saw her just often enough to monitor his drug usage. Although Alyssa tried to make sure he called his mother regularly, those calls had gotten shorter and less frequent.

Zachary entered the living room and knelt in front of her. She kicked off her slippers and extended her feet in his direction sighing with pleasure as he skillfully massaged them.

"Where did you get the tattoo on your backside?" The emblem seemed an easy way to broach the subject that had nagged at her for weeks now.

"Lady Jessica took me downtown one day and had it put on." He rubbed the balls of her feet with his thumbs.

"Did she tell you what that emblem means?" Although Alyssa had taken every available opportunity to pet Klark's soft hair, hold him in her arms, kiss him, she could never bring herself to show Zachary that kind of affection. She could tolerate his touch on her feet and her back because his strong fingers massaged away the aches and pains she felt more and more these days. But she never reached for him otherwise, and although she never locked it, the boy still slept in the cage in her dungeon.

"Yes, Mistress."

"She explained that the three crescent shapes represent the three BDSM threesomes?"

Zachary looked up, puzzled, but continued rubbing her feet. "She only mentioned one threesome: bondage and discipline, domination and submission, and sadism and masochism."

Alyssa reluctantly pulled her feet away. "No, there are three threesomes. Those, but also tops, bottoms, and switches, and, more importantly, safe, sane, and consensual." She put a hand on each of Zachary's cheeks. "I need you to think about what Jessica did to you. She violated doctor-patient boundaries; she enslaved you without consent, using methods that were neither safe nor sane; and then she abandoned you. Each of those is an ethical violation in itself, but combined they represent a magnitude of unconscionable behavior that requires retribution." Alyssa sat back on the sofa. She no longer considered Jessica a friend. If the woman still lived in Chicago, Alyssa might have tried some of the tactics she had used against the fiend who had killed Klark. Although she still had a lawsuit pending against that monster, she had finally abandoned her vendetta. Between school and watching over Zachary, she really had no time for further pursuit.

"What should I do, Mistress?" Zachary punctuated his question with a kiss on her toes. Although she tolerated the caress, his lips burned with the memory of how Klark's mouth felt against her feet.

"You should file a complaint against her with the Department of Professional Regulation. Even though she's moved to England, I'm sure she's kept her license here. You can make sure she never practices as a psychologist in Illinois again and I'm sure any disciplinary action here would get noticed by regulators in England as well."

"But, she didn't hurt me. She helped me."

Alyssa pulled her feet away from Zachary's lips, planted them on the floor and took his face in her hands. "No, boy.

She didn't help you. The pain she inflicted may have treated your depression. And you may benefit from the structure of a D/s relationship. But, she didn't need to enslave you or treat you like a dog to accomplish either of those."

Zachary's face crumpled and tears gathered at the corner of his eyes. Part of Alyssa wanted to pull him into her arms and comfort him, but the part of her who had adored Klark couldn't.

"She should have explained your options and choices regarding enslavement and allowed you to decide if you wanted to give yourself to anyone. She should never have even presented herself as a potential owner until after she had terminated your patient-therapist relationship, probably long after. Don't you understand? You're not anyone's property. You may choose to give yourself to an Owner, but you need to make that choice and you need to make such a decision with enough information to make it wisely." He closed his eyes. "Yes, Mistress. Thank you, Mistress." Alyssa sighed. He gave that answer because he knew he could never go wrong with it, not because he understood her words. "Go to your cage, boy. Take your journal with you. I want you to think about what you truly want from a relationship. I want you to think about all the things you might have missed out on by serving as a slave. Think about what you liked about serving Jessica, what's different about serving me, and then make a list of all the things you would want in a perfect Mistress."

"Yes, Mistress. Thank you, Mistress."

Z

Zachary sat cross-legged in his cage, the door open, his journal- -half filled with random thoughts scrawled in blue ink from a ballpoint pen -- open to a blank page. At the top he wrote: "My Perfect Mistress." He stuck the back of the pen in between his teeth. Did he have the right to make such a wish? Mistress Jessica treated him like a dog, because she believed he deserved no better. Mistress Alyssa treated him as if he were human, talking to him and soliciting his opinion. But she almost never touched him. He closed his eyes. Which did he want more.

He opened his eyes wide, his breath came quickly. What if he asked for both. Would Mistress consider him a greedy fool? Before he lost his courage, he wrote: "would embrace mysticism and spirituality, would enjoy watching the same movies, reading the same books, listening to the same music as i. She..." He paused. Mistress would read what he wrote. But he knew what he wanted. Someone closer to his own age. Someone he found attractive. Someone who would touch him, kiss him, make love to him. And not someone who would just let him lick her, as much as he enjoyed that.

Zachary wanted to experience sex. Intercourse. How it felt to penetrate a woman. He sprang to attention at the thought. He wanted to touch it. Mistress Alyssa had never forbidden him to masturbate, but she hadn't ever given him permission either.

Did his desire for a relationship with a woman mean he didn't want to be a slave? He still wanted a woman who would take control, who would tell him what to do, who would require the rituals that gave his life structure and meaning. He put the pen back on the paper.

"i believe i might do better as a submissive and not a slave, that i'm more suitable for D/s relationship that periodically may mimic slavery, but for the most part, is a mix of vanilla and Dominance/submission. As a submissive, i want my Dominant to see and appreciate me as a person first and a sub second. i want a Dominant who does not require the kind of stringent service that slavery requires, and who will give me more time to indulge in the various interests, pursuits, and vocations I have developed. These are not just things for Her to indulge or accommodate, they are things i need in my life and want to share with another. " Zachary paused, started to read what he had written, decided against it and plunged onward.

"i want to have a relationship with an egalitarian framework -- a democratic foundation that functions within an authoritarian context. i have come to realize this is diametrically opposed to an Owner/slave structured relationship. The relationship i seek might resemble more of the Authoritarian type of relationships we find in the vanilla world between teachers and students. The teacher/authority, has an advantage in Her skills and knowledge in certain realms, and imparts that knowledge to me within a context in which She makes the rules, and prescribes the rewards and punishments for following or breaking those rules. In this sense, both individuals share the same ultimate status as equals but each plays a different role for the mutual benefit of both."

Zachary sucked in his breath and let it out in one, long, slow exhale. What he had written violated everything Lady Jessica had believed about him. He held the page up, ready to tear it from the journal. Mistress claimed Lady Jessica had harmed him. Perhaps she was right. He continued where he had left off.

"Slavery transcends all contexts and requires a level of submission much more primal and stringent in nature. i no longer wish to give that level of submission. I realize that now. As a sub i want a relationship based on ongoing negotiation of when, where, and how i can fulfill my desires. And while my Dominant/mate will be the ultimate judge and authority in these negotiations, She will always take my desires into consideration and allow me to negotiate with Her rather than require me to sign into a permanent structure with a contract and that becomes forever nonnegotiable.

"Moreover, as a sub, i desire a Woman who finds me physically attractive and who i find physically attractive. i do not want a Woman who superficially accepts me intellectually and spiritually, but One who shares my passions, interests, and specific intellectual and spiritual philosophies. Thus, i would prefer She is socialist in political orientation, has knowledge of and actively pursues the occult, metaphysics, and various transcendental eastern philosophies. i want to find a Woman who does not just tolerate my interest in music and movies, but sincerely enjoys and understand them at the level i do.

"i want someone who will indulge my desire to live in a D/s structure that mimics slavery by establishing certain rituals and protocols of behavior that i am to follow. However, these rule and protocols will fulfill more utilitarian and fetish-orientated purposes, than slave- orientated. In essence, i desire a woman who is Dominant in the vanilla world, who can assist me with my deficiencies in that realm, and who is comfortable making the fundamental decisions in the relationship, but who will be open to the fact that i may grow and mature and develop in my vanilla competencies and will allow me more input and influence in making those decisions when i have proved that competency. This is a far cry from slavery. In fact, it mixes vanilla authoritarianism and D/s."

Zachary sighed, closed the notebook, put it down outside the cage, and set the pen down on top of it. He stared at it. Many of the thoughts he had written down had never crossed his mind before. But putting them on paper, made him understand how he had changed in the six months since Lady Jessica had abandoned him. He had to wonder how Lady Alyssa would react when she read what he wrote. Many of his requirements specifically ruled her out as a woman he would wish to give himself to. Although she had many pagan friends, she did not have any spiritual practices of her own. She never touched him. He didn't find her attractive and he didn't think she had any attraction for him. Although she allowed him to discuss some of the philosophical issues he found fascinating and which he held dear, he knew that she did not embrace them.

Zachary wrapped the blanket around himself and shivered. Still, Mistress had given him so much. She had rescued him from institutionalization. She had helped him realize how Lady Jessica had harmed him. She had given him the freedom to discover his own path. He pulled the notebook back into the cage and opened it again.

"This has been an exciting and enlightening journey, one from which i feel i have benefitted immensely and for which i could never begin to express my gratitude. i only hope You have derived some good from it. i so very much appreciate the time and energy You have invested in me and i will always be deeply grateful to You for that. Without a doubt You were instrumental in helping me come to a deeper realization of myself. "You know the old proverb: "Necessity is the mother of invention." The necessity of having to write a journal over the past several months, to share of myself with someone who required this expression as a part of my commitment to the relationship and Who required that i be ruthlessly honest with myself, has spurred me on to walk along the path of self-discovery and to take a deeper look at myself. i would have never done that with just any Dominant, so for that i am grateful to You." He closed the notebook and set it outside his cage once more. He hoped that last bit, which he meant with all sincerity, would mitigate the pain the rest of his words might cause Lady Alyssa.

Chapter Sixteen

Alyssa closed Zachary's journal and set it on the sofa beside her. On the one hand, she appreciated his honesty and gratitude. And she took some pride in helping him come to a better understanding of himself. On the other hand, although he could never take Klark's place, she enjoyed having a slave in her home again. She cringed at the thought of doing her own laundry and preparing her own meals. But Zachary's presence hadn't filled the empty place in her heart or her bed. In addition to encouraging Zachary to find a Mistress, perhaps she needed to invest some time in defining and seeking her perfect slave.

"Boy!"

He scurried in from the kitchen and knelt on the floor in front of her.

"I've read your journal."

"Yes, Mistress. Thank you, Mistress. May I speak, please."

Alyssa wondered what more he had to say. "Yes."

"I just want you to know, Mistress, how grateful I am for all the help you've given me, for the honor of serving you, for everything I have learned about myself and the lifestyle. I will always treasure the consideration you have shown me. I'm just sorry that I've disappointed you and that I can't offer myself to you."

"You haven't disappointed me." Alyssa manipulated numbers on the lock hanging from Zachary's neck, lining up the combination. "It has become obvious to me that you aren't the slave I seek. I think your service here has helped us both better define what we need from the lifestyle." She unhooked the hasp from the links and removed them from his neck. In some ways, releasing him offered relief from responsibility for someone so troubled. She only hoped she could help him find a better place. "You may continue to serve here until you find a place for yourself. And, moving out does not mean you have to sever ties. I have enjoyed both your service and your companionship. You are welcome here anytime as a friend."

Zachary's eyes filled with tears that glistened in the winter sunlight streaming through the window behind Alyssa. "Thank you so very, very much. You have no idea how much that means to me. You have been such a wonderful friend and I'm so very glad I do not have to give that up. Perhaps I can even come by occasionally and serve you until you find the one you seek."

Alyssa smiled. "I'd like that, boy. I really would. It gets terribly lonely here sometimes."

Z

With the help of an excellent reference from Lady Alyssa, Zachary used craigslist to find a part-time job with a cleaning service and a room for rent near campus. He hoped to enroll in the University at the start of the spring term, but he got fired from his job after only a month. Lady Alyssa helped him find another janitorial job, but that lasted only three weeks. The loading dock job ended after thirteen days and the grocery store fired him after six hours.

That afternoon, he took the bus up to Lady Alyssa's home,

even though she hadn't invited him to come visit. When she opened the door, she looked at him, her eyebrows pulled together, her lips pinched tight.

"I'm so very sorry to bother you, Mistress. But I got fired again. I feel like I want to crawl into bed and stay there and I hoped you would have time to flog me. Perhaps that would help me get a job I can keep."

Lady Alyssa looked him up and down. "Boy, when's the last time you've eaten?"

Zachary tried to remember, but couldn't. He shrugged.

She stood aside so he could enter her home. Once she closed the front door, he dropped to his knees and kissed her feet. "Thank you so much, Mistress, for allowing me the privilege of serving you."

"I think the first thing I'd better do is feed you. Then if you still think you need a flogging, we can go down to the dungeon."

Zachary admitted that his stomach felt rather empty. He removed his clothing, hung his jeans and tee shirt up in the front closet, and followed Lady Alyssa into the kitchen. She pulled a carton of leftover Chinese takeout from the fridge and handed it to him. He reached for the tableware drawer to grab a fork, but she put a hand over his.

"Warm it up in the microwave first."

"Yes, Mistress. Thank you, Mistress." Zachary heated the container for two minutes, took a fork, and shoveled noodles and bits of meat and vegetables into his mouth. He truly couldn't remember when he had last tasted food. He had scraped enough money together to pay his rent on the first and a week later for the cell phone that Lady Alyssa had reactivated when he moved out and he hadn't seen a paycheck since. In ten days his rent was due again.

"Slow down, boy. You'll make yourself sick."

"Yes, Mistress. Thank you, Mistress." Zachary lowered himself to his knees and chewed each fork full of food before swallowing. He tasted ginger, garlic, and red chili flavoring beef and broccoli. The spices woke up his senses and he smiled.

"Now, do you really think you need a beating or are you just hungry and discouraged?"

Zachary filled his mouth with another fork full of noodles. It tasted good. He knew if he had entered a depressive episode, food would not have any flavor. "I guess not. Thank you, Mistress."

"Why did you get fired this time?"

"I don't know. They said I showed disrespect to my supervisor. I didn't mean to call her mistress. She just acted so much like a Dominant, it slipped out."

Alyssa sucked in her breath and blew it out again. "I think we need to look at getting you some kind of disability income. I'm not sure you'll ever have what it takes to hold down a job. By the way, have you heard anything on your case against Jessica?"

Zachary scraped out the last of the spicy sauce from the container and licked it off the fork. "I got a notice a couple of days ago." Lady Alyssa had helped Zachary file a complaint against Dr. Richards with the Illinois Department of Professional Regulation. "I'm supposed to go in for a deposition. Apparently, they're also doing a deposition with Dora over the telephone." He put the empty container in the trash and the fork in the dishwasher.

"Well, hopefully she will corroborate your story." Alyssa headed toward the living room. "Let's go look online and see what we need to do to get you on disability."

"Yes, Mistress. Thank you, Mistress. But, may I clean your house first. I feel like you're taking such wonderful care of me and I'm not doing anything at all."

She laughed. "You clean, I'll research."

"Yes, Mistress. Thank you, Mistress."

Z

Horrified by Dora's summons to give a deposition over the telephone, Jessica used VoIP to call Zachary's cell phone. "What do you think you're doing, boy?"

"Mistress?"

"Yes, boy. What ever possessed you to file a complaint against me?" Jessica tried to keep her anger and fear out of her voice.

"I'm not a slave. I can't get a job. I don't want to be institutionalized." He sounded as if he might cry at any minute.

"You couldn't get a job before I took you in, either, remember. I gave you a place to live, structure to control your anxiety, and pain to manage your depression." She took a deep breath, trying to keep her emotions in check. "You came with me willingly and you signed an agreement to keep our relationship confidential."

"Lady Alyssa says I couldn't give informed consent because you were my therapist."

"She's behind this?" Jessica lost all control and yelled into the speaker. "She's the one who talked you into taking legal action against me?" She had thought Alyssa was her friend. How could she betray her like this?

"No." She heard Zachary take a deep breath. "Lady Alyssa stopped Dr. Johansson from having me committed. She let me serve her and she helped me figure out who I was and what I wanted. I'm not a slave. I don't want to serve a Mistress who treats me like an animal. I want to be with a woman who will love me and who will appreciate me. You never did." His voice broke and Jessica wondered what the hell he meant by all his blubbering. She suspected he was just repeating thoughts someone else, Alyssa apparently, had planted in his head. "You treated me worse than some people treat their dogs -- depriving me of sleep, caging me, making me eat off the floor."

"Zachary, I did that because you needed it. You needed the structure. You took refuge in that cage." She needed to remind him of all the ways she had helped him if she wanted to persuade him to drop his complaint.

"Lady Alyssa never locks the cage door. She lets me stay in there when I need to, but she's never imprisoned me. She never deprived me of sleep. She never made me eat off the floor."

"She didn't need to, I'd already done the work that helped you reach the place you needed to be at to serve." How dare Alyssa undermine her authority this way? Even if she had given Zachary to Alyssa, the woman had no business questioning Jessica's methodology. Jessica wished now she had never asked Alyssa to look after Zachary.

"I would have served you willingly if you'd offered me the choice. You didn't need to break me; you didn't need to treat me like an animal."

The resentment in his voice made it clear this conversation wasted her time. She would have to make the one phone call she had avoided since Dora received her subpoena.

"Your case will be thrown out. Have fun trying to find a therapist to treat you now -- no one wants a lawsuit-happy patient." Jessica terminated the connection and dialed Professor Lawrence's number.

Chapter Seventeen

Zachary thumbed through the typewritten pages on the table in front of him unable to understand how Dora could fabricate such lies. He always thought of her as his friend, his sister slave. She had encouraged him to start journaling in the first place. She had explained so many of the rituals he hadn't understood. She had pointed him to websites that explained the lifestyle and Mistress/slave dynamics.

"Zachary came to the house and begged Dr. Richards to take him in. He said he had lost his job and his landlord had evicted him. He claimed he had nowhere else to go." Dora's words cut through him. She had witnessed everything Lady Jessica had done those first weeks. She knew he had not gotten to the house on his own.

"Dr. Richards agreed that Zachary could sleep in the basement and do chores in exchange for room and board rather than see him living on the street. She recommended that if he needed to stay with her, he should find another therapist. Zachary refused to do this." Dora's words on the page blurred and Zachary wiped a hand across his eyes to clear his tears.

"This transcript of Isadora Jameson's deposition hardly supports your allegations," the attorney said. Zachary couldn't remember his name. "We don't appreciate frivolous complaints, Mr. Smith. Dr. Richards could take legal action against you for unwarranted harassment, slander, and a host of other charges."

Zachary held up the paper. "Lies." He sobbed. "All lies."

"Young man, it's bad enough that you filed these spurious accusations. But to claim Ms. Jameson has committed perjury in addition to flinging mud at Dr. Richards does you no credit. I suggest you leave now before I take it upon myself to initiate action against you for wasting this office's time."

Zachary managed to rise to his feet and, clutching his jacket, stumbled out of the conference room. He didn't know where to go or what to do. Filling the charges against Mistress had required an enormous effort and all his courage.

Z

Alyssa opened the front door to find Zachary, his lips blue, his hands red, standing on her porch with his jacket clutched to his chest. She grabbed his arm and dragged him inside. "Whatever were you thinking, boy, running around without wearing a coat when it's nearly freezing out?" She pulled him into the living room and flipped the switch to turn on the gas fire place. "Here, sit in front of the fire."

She pulled the afghan off the back of the sofa and wrapped it around his shoulders. "What happened downtown?"

"Dora lied and they won't pursue the case." He sobbed, his shoulders shaking. "She said I begged Dr. Richards to take me in because I got kicked out of my room. She claimed Dr. Richards told me to find another therapist. She said I lived in their house doing chores in exchange for room and board."

Alyssa sucked in air until her belly stuck out. She should

have realized that Dora would do anything to protect her Mistress, even lie. If this sent Zachary spiraling downward again, she could only blame herself. She had encouraged him to take action against Jessica.

Zachary looked up, tears streaming down his cheeks. "You believe me, don't you?"

She wrapped her arms around him. "Of course I do, you poor, dear boy. Dora is Jessica's slave. Apparently, she'll do anything she's told, even lie. For all we know, Jessica enlisted her old professor's help to get the case dropped."

Zachary buried his head against Alyssa's chest and she could feel the wetness of his tears through her sweater. She hesitated for a minute, but then ran her hand across the skin of his shaved head. "You can't let this keep you from moving forward, my dear. Jessica deserves punishment, but you can't let the fact that she won't get any keep you from going on with your life."

Alyssa's eyes widened grasping the significance of those words as they applied to her own circumstances. Nothing she did to his killer would bring Klark back. Instead of still mourning him, a year after his death, longing for something she could never have, she should move on and put the energy she had wasted on vengeance into finding a new pet. After all, she knew where to look. Through the FemDom group that gathered for Lady Gina's parties, she could meet at least half a dozen submissive males looking for an owner.

But that needed to wait. She stroked Zachary's head. First, she had to help this boy get back on his feet. She couldn't permit this setback to erode all the progress Zachary had made in breaking free from Jessica. "You've improved so much, my dear boy. You've come to terms with who and what you are. You no longer believe your only options are slavery or institutionalization. You understand your worth. Now you just need to find a woman who will appreciate it." Which really shouldn't be that difficult either. The boy was good looking, well built, obedient, and eager to serve.

Zachary shook his head without lifting it from Alyssa's cleavage. The movement of his head against her sensitive breasts stirred memories and feelings she hadn't experienced for a very long time. She tried to remember why she had decided a platonic relationship would better serve them best, but the reason alluded her now. Alyssa pulled Zachary closer, reminding herself how wonderful holding a firm, male body could feel.

She chastised herself for considering taking advantage of the boy while he grieved. Then she thought of all his journal entries about how much he loved it when Jessica allowed him to worship her orally, how much pride he took in making her come. Of course, Alyssa thought, I'm no Jessica. Still, if she allowed him to satisfy her long-forgotten needs, it probably would do wonders for his self-esteem. And she had a bond with Zachary beyond friendship. The boy had lived in her home for months, naked, on his knees. When he kissed her feet, he didn't do so perfunctorily. In fact, now that she thought about it, she had never asked or required him to do so. That seemed to come from his heart.

Alyssa put three fingers under Zachary's smooth chin and lifted his face so she could look into his pale blue eyes. "Whatever Jessica and Dora say about you, I know you're a wonderful boy who someday is going to make some woman very happy. You have an amazing mind, you're sweet, sensitive, and very obedient. If I were twenty years younger, I probably would have offered you my collar by now."

She touched her lips to his, to gauge his reaction. He closed his eyes and opened his mouth to her. When she thrust her tongue into his mouth, he sucked on it with a hunger that reminded her of his innocence. Alyssa moaned. The pleasure of a man's mouth against hers, the knowledge of his rather well-endowed attributes made her melt with longing. She needed to restrain herself and make sure she didn't make him do anything he didn't want to. With one hand on either side of his head, she pulled his mouth away from hers. "Zachary, you know that I'm not the right Mistress for you."

His lips turned down and the excitement in his eyes dimmed. "Yes, Mistress. Thank you, Mistress."

"But that doesn't mean I don't care about you. I do. I just want what's best for you and, unfortunately, that's not me. Right now, though, we're both alone. We both have needs. I would like it very much if you would meet my needs, boy, but only if that's what you want. Certain places a submissive should go only if he wants to. So I'm giving you a choice." Alyssa held her breath. Although she really shouldn't put her own self-esteem on the line this way, she couldn't help but wonder if she still had enough sex appeal for a boy young enough to be her son to want to bed her.

"Yes, Mistress. Thank you, Mistress. I understand. You have shown me such consideration. You have helped me so very much. I would find it such an honor if you would allow me to meet your needs. I will confess, I have wanted for a long time to worship you orally, but you never asked that of me."

Alyssa smiled. His words meant more to her than they should. She planted a kiss on Zachary's forehead. "You sweet boy. I shall take great pleasure in giving you that privilege. But, I'm offering you more -- if you want that."

Zachary pulled back, his eyes wide, his lips parted. "You would let me ... I mean, you want to ... are you ... I never thought..."

She laughed. She could accept his reaction as consent, but given his fragility, she needed more. "Stop stuttering, boy. We're going to go upstairs to my bedroom. You're going to give me a massage and you're going to worship me orally, as you put it. But you need to decide what happens after that. I haven't had a man inside me since Klark died and I miss that very, very much. Still, it's your choice. You need to let me know if that's something you want to do with me."

Zachary gasped. "Oh, yes, Mistress. More than any-thing. Thank you so very much, Mistress. I've never ... you know I'm ... I haven't ever ..."

"Yes, boy, I know you're a virgin." Alyssa smiled. His innocence did rather enhance his appeal. "And I think it's sweet that you're willing to give that to me." Alyssa kissed him again, this time biting his lower lip. She felt him slip toward the trance-like state of subspace. "Let's go, boy." She pushed against his shoulders to get to her feet and started toward the stairs. Zachary crawled after her on his hands and knees, the afghan trailing behind him onto the floor. At the bottom step she turned. "Put that away, turn off the fireplace and the lights, and you know better than to come upstairs with your clothes on."

"Yes, Mistress. Thank you, Mistress." Zachary scurried back toward the fireplace and Alyssa climbed the stairs to her bedroom, pulling her sweater over her head. She tossed it aside and scattered the rest of her clothing on the stairs and along the hallway.

By the time she reached the bedroom, Zachary had caught up with her and had gathered up her jeans, T-shirt, sweater, and bra. She sat on her bed, wearing only her pant-ies. After setting her clothing on the rocking chair, he knelt before her and removed her slippers. He kissed each one of her toes in turn, then licked the soles and tops of her feet. Alyssa sighed. Although she had always enjoyed his foot rubs, nothing compared to a submissive on his knees truly worshiping her feet.

Zachary went back to her toes, sucking on each one in-dividually, then taking all five of them in his mouth. Alyssa leaned down and kissed the top of his smooth head. She swung her legs up on the bed and rolled over on her stom-ach. He went into the bathroom and she heard the water running. When he returned with the massage oil, he had warmed both it and his hands.

Alyssa almost fell asleep under the wonderful soothing caress of his hands on her back and her legs. But, his touch also inflamed her need. She reached back and pulled the elastic of her panties down. He took the hint and slid the cotton fabric down her legs then kissed, nuzzled, and licked her rear end until she wiggled with desire. How could she have had this pretty boy in her home all this time and not taken advantage of what he offered?

Rolling over, Alyssa opened her legs. But Zachary reached for the massage oil and gently rubbed it into her breasts, her belly, and her arms. Panting, she couldn't wait any longer. A year had passed since she had any kind of sexual gratification. She planted one hand on the top of Zachary's head and pushed him toward her legs. He kissed his way down, starting with her breasts, his lips burning her skin. When he finally ran his tongue along the inside of her slit, Alyssa moaned and pressed her hips up to meet his face.

Jessica had taught the boy well. Within minutes, he brought her off and he kept licking until he made her come half a dozen times. Alyssa floated in ecstasy, her body feeling alive for the first time in so very, very long. She grabbed his ears, pulled his head up toward her shoulder and pushed him so he lay on his back. Unable to resist, she ran a finger along his length, enjoying the soft skin over blood-engorged flesh. "You ready, boy."

"Oh, yes, Mistress. Thank you so very, very much."

Alyssa laughed. She straddled the boy and lowered herself down on his lovely hardness. She paused a moment, enjoying the wonderful, full sensation and the look of absolute bliss on the boy's face. She slid up and down and the boy ran his hands along her legs to her rear, driving her wild with his tender caress. She came hard and the boy gasped.

"Oh, Mistress, please. I can't hold back."

His plea jolted Alyssa out of her post-orgasmic stupor.

She rose up and let him flop to one side. "Oh yes, you can. You'll come when I give you permission, and not before."

"Yes, Mistress. Thank you, Mistress."

She waited until the boy's breathing became more even before taking him inside her again. Twice more she stopped and pulled him out of her to prevent him from coming too soon. He needed to appreciate the privilege granted by a woman who allowed him to come inside her. After she had used him to bring herself off another half a dozen times, she decided the boy had earned his reward. "You may come now, boy."

"Oh, thank you so much, Mistress." He grabbed onto her legs and thrust his hips up into her, making her come one more time before he screamed out.

When he stopped spasming and slipped out of her, Alyssa rolled over on her back. She really could have curled up with him and fallen asleep in absolute contentment. But he needed to learn protocol. She pushed his head toward her legs. "Clean up your mess, boy."

"Yes, Mistress. Thank you, Mistress. That was so very wonderful." He crawled down and lapped and sucked all his ejaculate out of her and made her come again.

Chapter Eighteen

When Alyssa opened her front door, she had to grab onto it for support. The tiny blonde stood on the front porch, a canvass duffle bag at her feet, stomping to ward away the cold. Big wet flakes of snow melted when they touched the skin of her face and the leather jacket that she wore over worn blue jeans.

"Lady Alyssa, please forgive the intrusion, but I wanted to talk to Zachary and apologize for what I've done to him," Dora said. "I was hoping you would know where to find him."

Alyssa raised one eyebrow, her anger assuaged by the promise in one of Dora's words. "Apologize?"

Dora stared at her feet. "Mistress insisted I lie in the deposition," she whispered so softly, Alyssa could barely hear her over the wind blowing in from the lake.

That confession elicited no surprise. That Dora now sought forgiveness seemed improbable and confusing. But Alyssa saw no need to keep the girl freezing outside on the porch until she learned more. She opened the door wider and moved out of the opening. Dora picked up her duffle and stepped inside. As soon as Alyssa closed the door, Dora dropped to her knees. "I'm so sorry for what I did, Lady Alyssa. I obeyed my Mistress, even though I knew it was wrong."

For the first time, Alyssa noticed the naked skin under Dora's chin. The ramifications of that missing collar caused her to feel sorrow, joy, fear, and gratitude all at once. She had to steel herself to speak. "You've left her?"

"Yes, Ma'am. I pulled the links of my collar apart with pliers, packed some clothing," she pointed to the duffle, "and used Mistress' credit card to buy a ticket home." She put her face in her hands and her shoulders shook. "I love Mistress with all my heart and soul. I only wanted to serve her and I was proud to wear her collar."

Alyssa stepped up to Dora and patted her head. The poor dear, how could Jessica put her in such an awkward position? The girl wrapped her arms around Alyssa's legs and sobbed into her knees.

"But I knew Zachary had never consented to what Mistress did. At the time I believed she had chosen the best path for him, given his condition. But then I learned that he had filed a complaint, that she had betrayed her position as his therapist. When she made me lie..."

Stroking Dora's hair, Alyssa took a deep breath. The girl had shown an amazing amount of courage walking away from her owner. And Zachary needed to hear that Jessica had lied and even Dora didn't trust her anymore. "What will you do now?"

"I hoped I could stay with you until I found Zachary and contacted the Professional Regulation Department to ask if I could given another deposition in person. Then I planned to go back to Decatur. I can live with my folks until I find a job."

"Will you tell the Department the truth this time?" Zachary stepped into the living room and Alyssa wondered how long he had listened to Dora's confession. He showed a great deal of restraint given how hard he had taken Dora's betrayal.

"Oh, Zachary. I'm so sorry." Dora released Alyssa and crawled over toward him, but Zachary dropped to his own knees.

"You can't kneel before me, Dora. I'm just a slave like you."

Dora paused and rested her rear on her heels. "At least you've found a new Mistress, I'm alone." Alyssa heard such a mournful plea in the girl's tone, her heart went out to Dora.

"No, I don't belong to Lady Alyssa. She's allowing me to serve her until I find someone who wants me." He grimaced and Alyssa wished they were more compatible. The boy certainly had a lot to offer in so many ways.

"Can you ever forgive me for what I've done, Zachary."

The boy stared at Dora's tear-streaked face for a long while before he spoke. "If you tell the truth, yes, I can forgive you."

Alyssa smiled. At least Zachary still had his friend, his sister slave. And if she did repudiate her prior testimony and corroborate Zachary's report of Jessica's abuses, the woman probably would never practice in the U.S. again.

Z

The disability income that Mistress Alyssa had worked with his therapist to obtain for him gave Zachary enough for rent, books, and bus fare to go to visit her every weekend. She let him clean her house, cook food for her to reheat during the week, and worship her. Although he enjoyed serving her every way she permitted, he liked pleasing her sexually best. She tasted so wonderful -- not the honey sweetness of Lady Jessica, more like the richness of French vanilla. Her skin felt so soft under his mouth and his hands and he could not believe he had spent thirty-two years of his life without ever knowing how wonderful it felt to put himself inside a woman.

He had gotten much better at lasting as long as she wanted-ed. He learned to masturbate several times before he took the bus to her house -- that helped immensely. Mostly, he found watching her use him to pleasure herself until she came again and again -- she could get off so many more times than Lady Jessica had -- so wonderful he just stayed hard for as long as she wanted. Sometimes she rode him like she had the first time. Others, she lay on her back and made him get on his side perpendicular to her and move his hips so he plunged in and out. Always, she let him come inside her and then made him lick her clean.

During the week, Zachary attended classes in psychology and philosophy at the university. Since he had missed the start of the term, he only audited the classes. But, his disability status entitled him to reduced tuition and he hoped to take some classes for credit in the fall.

Mistress let him take enough food home each week so he could put the money he would spend on groceries toward school. She showed him several online sites where he could look for a Mistress of his own, but Zachary found contentment in serving Lady Alyssa, and studying. He really didn't believe he could find someone who would appreciate him as much as Lady Alyssa did, anyway.

"If you won't look for an owner online, then I'll just have to put you on display." Mistress drained the last of the wine from her glass and set it back down on the table. "Hurry and clean up the dishes, tonight we're going to a party."

"But, I don't have any appropriate clothing, Mistress."

"You won't need any clothing once we get to the party, silly boy. It's a play party. Now clean up so you can help me get into my corset and pack my toys."

After he followed her instructions and filled a small black suitcase with floggers, single tails, paddles, leather cuffs, and a fifty- foot length of rope, Zachary followed Mistress up to her bedroom. She had him remove her clothing and then pointed him to a drawer in the oak chest that stood opposite her bed. From this he removed a beautiful, brocade black corset with gold threads making a paisley pattern. She held this against her breasts and belly while Zachary threaded the laces through the eyelets in the back. He pulled the strings tight while she smoothed the fabric back until she said: "Good. That's perfect. Tie the laces into a bow." When he had finished, she added, "get my stockings."

Zachary found a pair of black, nylon stockings in Mistress' hosiery drawer and bunched one up so she could stick her toes into it. He drew the silky sheer fabric up her leg and attached the garters. Impulsively, he kissed the inside of her thigh and she rewarded him with a pat on the head. Since she had started allowing him to please her sexually, Mistress showed him much more affection and he so appreciated that.

When he had attached her second stocking, Mistress had him put a silky black thong and a straight black leather skirt on her. She stepped into pair of patent leather high heels and Zachary sat back and gasped. "Mistress, you look so very beautiful."

"Thank you, boy, but I'm sure you'll find much prettier Dominas at the party tonight." She headed out of the room and Zachary followed.

"I don't think that's possible, Mistress." She laughed. "Put your clothes on, boy, and get my coat." Zachary followed Mistress out to the driveway to her new Prius, purchased only two months ago. He helped her into the driver's seat, put her toy bag into the hatchback, and climbed into the passenger seat. They drove for almost an hour before Mistress parked at the curb behind a long line of cars. He carried the suitcase and walked three feet behind her, following Mistress a block down the sidewalk and up a long set of cement stairs to a covered porch with tall white columns on either end.

Mistress rang the bell and the door opened. When they stepped inside, a naked boy took Mistress' coat and hung it up in the closet. "You can put your things there." The boy pointed to six-foot tall wooden shelves with cubbyholes many of which already had clothing stuffed in them. Zachary stripped down, folded his jeans and T-shirt, and set them on top of his tennis shoes and jacket inside one of the cubbies. Mistress put a dog collar around his neck and attached a leather leash to it. Following Mistress down the stairs, her suitcase in his hand, brought back memories of Lady Jessica's dungeon. But this room had warm carpet on the floor and wood covering the walls. He couldn't see bare cement anywhere. Mistress led him over to a St. Andrew's cross, snapped her fingers, and pointed to the floor. Zachary dropped to his knees. He hadn't had a depressive episode since Dora returned and he didn't really need any pain therapy. But, he supposed if Mistress wanted to hurt him, he couldn't see any harm. He'd never had anyone else watch him taking a whip or a flogger.

"Wait here." She left him and he watched her greeting ladies who attended the party. Zachary saw a number of other naked boys including one lying flat on his back on a padded table along one wall of the large room. Someone stood over him, using a Wartenburg wheel and a tiny flogger to abuse his cock. Zachary cringed, remembering when Lady Jessica did that to him. Another boy stood with his hands in cuffs hanging from the ceiling.

He saw several younger and many older women. Some wore corsets, one woman had on a latex dress, a few just wore plain black outfits. He found a number of them quite unattractive. Although Mistress had thirty or forty pounds on Lady Jessica, some of the women at the party made Mistress Alyssa seem tiny. He saw tall willowy women he didn't find appealing either. He really didn't know what kind of woman attracted him. It had more to do with how she behaved and what she thought, perhaps, than how she looked. He had loved Lady Jessica. As much as it hurt to admit, given what she had done to him, he had loved her. Perhaps some of his pain came from the fact that in the end she abandoned him.

None of the women he saw held any particular appeal. He wondered if Mistress Alyssa planned on requiring that he serve any of them. He thought about the toys in the suitcase. She hadn't hurt him for a very long time, months, in fact. He still took klonopin and paroxetine. And a steady, predictable routine combined with using his MP3 player to avoid interaction with anyone he didn't know, kept Zachary's anxiety at bay and had not experienced a depressive episode since before Lady Alyssa made love to him the first time.

When she returned to the cross, Mistress stood in front of him with her feet spread apart. Zachary leaned forward and planted a kiss on the top of each foot between the leather and her ankle. When he brought his head back up to her waist, she whispered in his ear: "See anyone you'd like to play with, boy?"

"Only you, Mistress." He knew she enjoyed hurting him and he saw no other woman who he wanted to give that pleasure to.

"Alright, boy. I won't put a tag on you, then. But I'm going to play with one of the other toys first. You can serve as my party slave. You'll hand me the toys I ask for, clean them when I'm done playing, and wipe off the cross when I'm through with it. Understand?"

"Yes, Mistress. Thank you, Mistress." Zachary was relieved that she apparently didn't intend to hurt him. He had never enjoyed the pain, although he knew when he needed it.

"Look at no one else. Do not speak to anyone. Do not speak to me unless I ask you to or give you permission."

"Yes, Mistress. Thank you, Mistress."

She unclipped his leash and walked over to one of the older boys who had on a leather collar with a three- by five-inch paper tag hanging from it. She clipped her leash to his collar and led him over to the cross. "Cuffs."

Zachary lay the suitcase flat, unzipped it, and extracted

four leather cuffs. He handed them to Mistress one at a time, and she fastened them to the boy's wrists and ankles. A head taller than Mistress, he had thick black and grey hair that grazed his shoulders and only receded a little from his forehead. Muscular with equipment that looked much smaller than Zachary's own, the boy's face, neck, and forearms seemed slightly darker than the rest of his skin. Zachary wondered if Mistress found him attractive and why.

Mistress clipped the boy's wrists and ankles to rings on the cross, stepping up on the three-inch high brace that supported the cross to reach high enough. "Deerhide."

Zachary reached into the suitcase and extracted the softest flogger of those she had selected to bring with. Mistress started out throwing the flogger gently against the boy's shoulders, her wrist moving in a figure eight. This turned the boy on and by the time Mistress requested the buffalo hide flogger he had gotten almost as large as Zachary could.

After she started raising welts with the flogger, Mistress asked for her four-foot whip. She striped the boy's rear, his shoulders, his legs. When each stroke touched his skin, the boy rose up on his toes and clenched his fists. Mistress waited until he dropped back to the flat of his feet and opened his fingers before throwing again.

Zachary admired her precision. He had never watched anyone get a beating before and he found the experience enlightening. When Mistress finally took the boy down from the cross and sat down on the carpet with him in her arms, Zachary found himself wishing to trade places. Mistress stroked the boy's hair, caressed the welts across his back, and kissed him. He wrapped his arms around her waist and clung to her, shaking.

Zachary collected the floggers and the whip, wiped them down, and sprayed the cross with alcohol before wiping it clean with paper towels. When he returned from putting the spray bottle and paper towel roll back on the table in the center of the room and dropping the used towels in the garbage, he heard them talking quietly.

"No, the boy's just under my protection for now. I don't own him and have no intention of collaring him. He needs someone closer to his own age," Mistress said.

"Didn't you have a pet for a long time? I seem to remember you bringing someone else with you." The boy still had his arms around Mistress' waist and his head against her shoulder.

Zachary resisted an urge to pull the man away from his Mistress. Not knowing what else to do, he dropped to his knees next to the suitcase.

"I've not attended one of these parties for more than a year. You must have been coming for a long time."

"I corresponded with a woman online who recommended me to Lady Gina. I noticed you the first time I attended and to be honest I've returned each time hoping you would play with me. I almost gave up, I hadn't seen you in so long. But, Lady Gina called me this morning and said you might attend tonight. Did your pet leave you?"

"No. A drunk driver killed him about a year ago."

The boy lifted his head. "I'm so very sorry, Ma'am. When you think you're ready to look for a replacement, may I ask for the opportunity to present myself."

Mistress smiled at the boy. "That's why I'm here tonight. To see what's available."

Zachary cringed. If Mistress found someone else she wouldn't need him to serve her anymore.

"Serving you would be such an honor. I've heard many in the community speak highly of you."

Mistress raised one eyebrow. "If you knew enough to ask about me, why didn't you know what became of my pet?"

He shook his head. "No one really talked about it. They would just mutter about how sorry they felt for you. Of course, I never asked directly. I just let people know I would appreciate an introduction."

Zachary found his breathing had gotten ragged and his pulse was racing. He tried to analyze his reaction to the conversation. On the one hand, he understood that Mistress didn't believe she suited him and he really wanted her to find someone who could make her happy. On the other, he didn't know what he would do if she found another pet and no longer needed him to come clean her house and meet her other needs every weekend. He deliberately breathed out and in, out and in until he calmed himself. Mistress knew best. If she found another pet she would, he hoped, not abandon him. She had complained bitterly about Lady Jessica doing just that. Perhaps she would help him find the right Mistress.

His own thoughts tumbling about in his head, he had lost track of the conversation between Mistress and the boy. Mistress snapped her fingers at Zachary. "Pay attention, boy. I asked for pen and paper. Go find me some."

"Yes, Mistress. Sorry, Mistress." Zachary scurried up the stairs and asked the naked boy at the door. The boy gave him a tag like those which hung from many of the collars in the dungeon and a felt-tipped pen. On one side, the tag had check boxes and a list: "flogging, single tail, CBT, needles, knife play, candle wax, bondage." He brought the card to Mistress.

"Here's my phone number and e-mail." She wrote both on the back of the tag and handed them to the boy. "Get in touch with me next week and we'll get together to continue this conversation."

"Yes, Ma'am. Thank you so very much, Ma'am."

Zachary looked at the boy and wondered if he realized just how lucky he was to have such a wonderful Mistress interested in him. He thought about sharing his opinion, but then decided if the boy had come to the party looking for Lady Alyssa he must appreciate what she had to offer.

Z

Jessica stared at the papers in her hands until her vision blurred. Since Dora left, she had stopped wearing mascara. Even though she bought the best brand of waterproof, her tears invariably smeared it by the end of the day. Now she couldn't even follow Dora back to the States. The Illinois Department of Professional Regulation has revoked her licenses to practice medicine due to "unethical, unprofessional, dishonorable, and immoral conduct and gross negligence." In addition, the regulators demanded she pay a five-thousand-dollar fine. She crumpled the paper and tossed it at the wall. Her hands trembled and her she could feel the heat creeping up her cheeks.

Despite Professor Lawrence's attempts to get the case squashed, Dora's recantation of her previous deposition supported Zachary's complaint and the Department's prosecutors had sought the maximum penalties. The Department would forward the information to the University here and she probably would lose her research grant.

Without Dora, her life had no joy. Without her career, it had no meaning. Jessica leaned her arms on her desk, rested her head against them and wept until she could not breathe. She wondered if she should try her father's solution.

"Stop feeling sorry for yourself." Jessica picked up her head and wiped away her tears with the back of her hand. Whatever happened to her career, she didn't need to worry about money. She had turned down dozens of offers from men she met at the clubs -- if necessary she could return to working as a ProDom. Unhampered by academic requirements or grant restrictions, she could continue her research with her clients. When she broke new ground in treatment for depression, they would have to let her practice again.

Chapter Nineteen

Zachary took his cup of coffee over to the service counter and added sugar and cream. He had taken to spending Thursday afternoons at the Chase Café near campus. They let him sit at one of the tables and study his philosophy books for the price of a cup of coffee. And Sally, one of the baristas, always gave him a free refill. He settled at a table near the window and studied his text.

The scent of roses tickled his nostrils and he looked up to see a woman walk by. She wore a black leather skirt, knee-high boots that laced up the back, and a silky black blouse. He watched her order a latte and admired the way her long legs carried her gracefully across the room. She had short curly black hair that framed a pale face, lips painted bright red, and several gold earrings in each ear.

When she sat down at a table, she pulled a paperback out of the large leather bag she carried on her shoulder. She opened it to where a marker stuck out near the middle. Zachary recognized the cover of the book: "Beyond Good & Evil: Prelude to a Philosophy of the Future," by Friedrich Nietzsche and Walter Kaufmann.

He wished he could find a Mistress like her -- beautiful, intelligent, philosophical. Slurping down the rest of his coffee, he went back to Sally to get his refill. He almost dropped his cup when he passed the table where the woman sat. One of the earrings in her left ear was the emblem. The most beautiful woman he could want to serve had walked into his favorite hang out and proclaimed her Dominance.

As usual, Sally made a production of making sure no one observed her refilling his cup. Normally Zachary just muttered thanks and scurried back to his table. This time he had to walk very carefully with his cup to get to the service counter without spilling coffee. Even though Sally knew to leave room for cream, Zachary's hands shook so much he had to carry the saucer with both hands. Even then, when he reached for the cream pitcher, he noticed he had splattered coffee on his shirt. He was getting himself all worked up over nothing. Such a pretty Mistress probably already had a pet or two and would have no use for someone with as many problems as he had.

Grasping the counter for support, Zachary tried to figure out what he should do. He reached into his pocket for his cell phone to call Lady Alyssa and ask her. But he knew what she would say. He just didn't know if he had the courage. With difficulty, he managed to get sugar and cream into his cup and carry it over to his table without attracting notice. Stirring his coffee, his book untouched by his hand, he stared at her. *She probably has a pet. And why would she want someone like me who can't even keep a job. She's probably just reading that book because it's required.* But Zachary knew of only one higher level course that required reading Nietzsche, the one he planned to take next term. No one took it unless they had a fairly strong background and interest.

He lifted his cup to his lips, but put it back when he realized his coffee had gotten cold. *If he didn't approach her, he might never see her again. But, how could he? What did he have to offer someone so beautiful?* Lady Alyssa's words played back in his head to taunt him. *... you're a wonderful boy who someday is going to make some woman very happy. You have an amazing mind, you're sweet and sensitive.*

The Domina put the marker back between the pages and stuck the book into her bag and Zachary saw his dream potentially walking out of his life forever. Before she could get up to leave, Zachary flung himself across the room and squatted next to her chair, keeping his head below hers. "Excuse me, Ma'am. I couldn't help noticing your earring." His stared at the blue and black tiles of the floor, trying to keep from trembling wishing he had curbed the impulse to confront her. But he couldn't exactly back out now. "I was wondering, if you might have any need of a very obedient, well-trained boy who finds you exceedingly attractive and would love to serve someone who appreciates Nietzsche."

Zachary waited, trembling, for her to send him away, perhaps call the police. He wanted to run home, and crawl into bed, and never emerge. But instead of angry words, he only heard a beautiful musical chime. He finally realized the sound caressing his ears was her laughter.

She put her hand under his chin and lifted his face forcing him to look into the most intense pair of green eyes he had ever seen. "You're kind of cute. What's your name, boy?"

He wanted to kneel and kiss her feet, but knew he couldn't do that in public. "Zachary, Ma'am."

"I'm Lady Elinor." She patted the chair nearest hers. "Tell me a little more about yourself, Zachary."

"Oh, thank you so very much, Ma'am." Zachary stood up and sat in the chair, his hands folded in his lap. He couldn't believe she was willing to talk to him. What if she liked him enough to offer him her collar? How heavenly. He took a deep breath. One step at a time, one step at a time, he told himself. "What would you like to know, Ma'am?"

ZZZ

Acknowledgments

Many thanks to those all those who have contributed to my success by sharing their knowledge, skills, and support, including: boy robin, who served me well while he was under my protection; brad, who had more influence than he'll ever understand; Cindy, my proofreader, editor and best friend; Conrad Hodson; david, James; Deborah Dixon; and all the friends who encouraged me to persevere.

Other novels by Korin I. Dushayl include:

Broken

some things can never be fixed

Given a choice between slavery and ostracization, Jessica chooses to kneel naked before her department head so she can continue studying for her PhD in psychology. That decision takes her down a dark path to abuse, exploitation, and torment of both her body and her spirit.

Korin Dushayl "writes with authority and compassion about those who live within the lifestyle. *Broken* and *Shattered* explore issues including finding and initiating a submissive partner, informed consent, and the difference between dominating someone and exploiting their needs."

Elizabeth Coldwell
author, anthologist, magazine editor
(Read the first few pages starting on page 143)

Playing With Dolls

"a must read for anyone who ever had

to learn how to be comfortable in their own skin"

Jesse enjoys playing with dolls and wearing girls' clothing and everyone from his parents, teachers, friends and neighbors assumes he will grow up gay. As an adult the burden of those assumptions hampers his ability to come to terms with his sexuality"

Korin I. Dushayl "has accomplished something remarkable here, crafting a story that works on all levels —

educating, arousing, inspiring, empowering, and (most importantly) emotionally connecting with the reader."
Sally Bibrary, Bending the Bookshelf

Buy it in Print

or E-Book

Choices

Must Linda's sexual awakening destroy her marriage?

From fairy tales to modern legal tradition, society demands we love exclusively, even though many only find happiness with multiple partners. Linda finally confronts long neglected sexual needs when Phil forces himself on her in Chicago. But back in Portland, her husband's insistence on monogamy compels her to choose between his limitations and her own insatiable desires.

Buy it in Print

or E-Book

For more information visit
http://transgressivewriter.com

Chapter One

Jessica Richards picked her way through the wet grass, trying to keep the heels of her Louis Vuitton boots from sinking into the turf. She made her way to the gaping hole next to her mother's grave, clutching a silk handkerchief she could use to dab at her eyes and prevent tears from streaking her makeup. When she finally reached the graveside, the fake grass under the canopy allowed her to stop tiptoeing.

The moment she took her seat and crossed her long legs, a short, balding man in a cheap raincoat and worn, mud-spattered loafers spoke. "Dearly beloved, we gather today to mourn the passing of," he paused to check a piece of paper tucked into his prayer book. "Francis 'Frank' Richards, devoted husband and father." With that last word, he looked at Jessica with an expression he probably intended as sympathetic, but that set her teeth on edge. She had never seen the man before and he had no clue what kind of man her father had been.

For the past several days, she had endured condolences tinged with scorn from anyone who read the news reports about the well-known investor found by his housekeeper with a pistol in his hand and a bullet in his brain. Jessica shut out the Reverend's deep, sonorous voice, focusing instead on the leather scent of her trench coat, the softness of its cashmere lining against her skin, and the drip of the rain on the canvas tent above the plastic folding chairs.

When he finally finished droning on, Jessica stood and stepped closer to the polished mahogany casket adorned with a spray of white lilies. She put her leather gloves in front of her lips, careful not to smudge her lipstick, and touched the casket. An errant tear trickled down her cheek and her handkerchief came away with a black smudge from her mascara.

Jessica pressed her lips together and stepped away. Walking back to the limousine, she could hear the creak of the gears as the grave diggers lowered the casket into the ground. The thunk as it came to rest at the bottom of the concrete vault reminded her that losing both her parents before her twenty-third birthday would define the rest of her life. She pressed the handkerchief below both eyes, hoping to avoid additional smears.

Before she climbed into the Town Car, Jessica looked around at the meager turnout. Only her father's attorney, Louis Foster, her friend Alyssa Volker, a few of her father's associates, and the housekeeper had braved the drizzly September morning to venture just north of Chicago to Graceland Cemetery. Dozens more had turned out for her mother's funeral a year ago. But Lenora Richards' life had ended in a fiery crash on the Edens Expressway, rather than at her own hand.

Except for Louis, everyone hurried to their own cars, sparing Jessica additional platitudes. Louis followed her into the Town Car and rode back to the house with her. Although he didn't speak, he held her gloved hand in both of his bare ones.

Just before the car pulled into the long, circular driveway of the house on Lake Shore Drive, Jessica swallowed hard. Although she had known him since childhood, she had no clue how to open a discussion about her finances with her father's attorney. She closed her eyes. That conversation, she supposed, could wait. Now, she needed to play hostess if anyone insisted on prolonging the funeral by visiting the house.

Fumbling in her Versace handbag, Jessica found her compact. To her dismay, despite her choice of a waterproof formula, her tears had created a ring of mascara around her green eyes. In addition, the rain had frizzed her normally straight black hair. Knowing she couldn't do anything about her hair without gel and a dryer, she moistened her handkerchief with her tongue and tried to scrub some of the black mess from the pale skin under her dark lashes.

When the battered pickup truck finally pulled away, Jessica eased her blue Mercedes-Benz convertible into a metered spot in front of the dingy coffee shop on Halsted Street. She put the car in park, turned off the engine, and gripped the steering wheel until her hands stopped shaking. After ignoring her phone calls for the past three weeks, Louis had finally had his secretary summon Jessica to meet him in this horrid neighborhood. Jessica took a deep breath, climbed out of the car, and used the clicker to set the alarm.

She hesitated before pushing open the door to the coffee shop, wondering if the secretary had given her the wrong address. Then she saw Louis huddled in a booth at the back of the restaurant, his hands wrapped around a chipped coffee mug.

"Whatever possessed you to select this dump as a meeting place?" Jessica asked, sliding onto the plastic seat across the stained melamine table.

"Get used to it. This is the best you can afford these days." He practically spat the words out.

Jessica stared at Louis Foster's lined face, pale against black hair trimmed above his ears, with gray streaks at his temples. She had always thought of him as more like an uncle than her father's attorney, and his tone stung as much as his words confused her.

A busty, pink-uniformed waitress approached the table, a coffee pot in one hand. At least a size fourteen, Jessica thought with scorn.

"You want coffee, honey?"

"I don't suppose you can serve me a mocha?"

Louis turned the cup in front of Jessica over. "She'll have regular joe, just like me."

The waitress filled Jessica's cup. "Anything else?"

"Thanks, no," Louis said.

Jessica found a dish of plastic creamer containers next to the metal napkin holder under the grimy window. She emptied two into her cup and poured in sugar from the metal-topped dispenser. "You going to tell me what's going on?"

He waved his hand across the table. "Isn't it obvious? You're broke."

"Louis, please stop kidding around." Jessica took a sip and grimaced. "This stuff is awful."

"Unless you've got someone to buy you better coffee, you're going to have to learn to live with it. And without credit cards. I've had to cancel all the ones your father gave you as of this morning."

Jessica tightened her grip on the coffee cup until the heat penetrating the ceramic hurt her hand.

"Your father spoiled you rotten, despite my advice to let you learn how to survive on your own. Well, he and the money are gone — you have no one to give you credit cards or pay all your bills. You need to make your own car and insurance payments or sell it. You'll have to come up with rent, groceries. No one will take care of you anymore." Louis stared at the liquid in his cup.

Jessica's looked inside her own coffee cup. It looked like a latte but tasted like dirt. Unable to comprehend his anger and bitterness toward her, she tried to at least make sense of Louis' words. "How am I supposed to pay my rent? I've got at least five more years of graduate school before I can expect any kind of income. My father promised to pay for my education. I could see him setting up a trust to make sure I finished school, but surely he made allowances for living expenses as well?"

Louis looked up at her. Dark shadows rimmed his brown eyes. "Your parents already paid for four years of college and carried you for the past three years of graduate school. With what they've shelled out already, you'd think you could get some kind of job. There's no trust fund. If you want to continue graduate school, you'll have to figure out how to pay the tuition. You're busted."

"You keep saying that. What do you mean?" Jessica lifted the cup to her lips, sniffed it, and set it back down. Louis seemed angry at her and she had no idea why.

"You do know why your father ate his own gun?"

"He finally succumbed to grief for my mother."

Louis snorted. "Surely you get some exposure to the outside world from your hallowed academic halls. Haven't you paid any attention to what's going on in the stock market?"

Jessica shook her head. Her father had repeatedly told her to concentrate on her studies and not worry about money — that he would always take care of her. She had never held a job, written a check, or filled out a credit card application.

"Well, I'll make it simple then: he lost everything. All the volatile high tech stock he invested in tanked." Louis picked up his cup, drained it, and plunked it down on the table. "You're destitute." The cold, unemotional way he spoke those words punched Jessica in the gut. She almost wanted the anger back. "The house is on the market, but with real estate prices where they are and all the stuff your parents added that no one will pay for, you'll be lucky to get enough to pay off the mortgage."

Jessica blinked rapidly to keep her tears at bay. "But what about the money from Mom's estate?"

"Gone. All you've inherited is debt."

"How could you let this happen? My father promised to support me while I worked on my PhD. I'm having a hard enough time with the course work and my thesis as it is — I'll never make it if I have to get a job."

Louis shrugged. "Then I guess you'll have to quit." He

sighed and his voice softened. "Look, Jessica, I didn't let this happen. I've been struggling for the past three weeks trying to figure out where all the money went. I can't even find enough to pay off your father's debts. And, given the state of his affairs, I've essentially been working for free." He ran his fingers through his hair. "I warned him about ..." He shook his head as if trying to clear his head. "Doesn't matter now."

Jessica stared at him, afraid that if she tried to speak she would burst into tears.

"Sorry, hon." Louis reached across the table and patted Jessica's hand. "I know this is hard for you to accept, that's why I dragged you down here so the reality would sink in. You need to understand sooner, rather than later, the gravity of your financial situation or you're just going to get yourself in a world of trouble. I've tried to straighten out the mess your father left, but I just can't afford to help you anymore."

Louis slid out of the booth, stood, and tossed three one dollar bills on the table. "Coffee's on me, but you're on your own now. Gotta go." He walked out the front door before Jessica could decide if she wanted him to come back.

The waitress stepped up to the table with the coffee pot in her hand. "Ya want a refill, sugar?" She grabbed the money and stuck it in the pocket of her apron.

Jessica didn't look up. The waitress represented everything she didn't want in her life: double-digit dress size, cheap clothing, menial job, no education. "No, thanks." She waited until the waitress' white sneakers disappeared from view, put her elbows on the table, and buried her face in her hands. Her shoulders shook, but she managed, except when she gasped for air, to keep her sobs silent.

Jessica unlocked the mailbox in the foyer of her apartment

and pulled out envelope after envelope. They all had yellow stickers with her address printed on them plastered over the plastic windows showing the address of the now-empty house on Lake Shore Drive. She had gotten out of the habit of checking her mailbox regularly, since all of the bills went to her father and most of the rest of her mail consisted of credit card offers and flyers from nearby stores. I bet no one will offer me credit cards now.

Once inside her apartment, she sat down at her desk and stared at the pile of envelopes. Hands shaking, she reached for the Samurai sword letter opener and sliced through the top of the first one. Her three-hundred-eighty-five-a-month car payment, ten days late, required an additional fifty-dollar penalty. Monthly insurance premiums for the car cost a hundred-and-forty dollars. Those two payments alone were almost as much as her rent.

Jessica dropped the letter opener on the pile of unopened envelopes and rested her chin on her open palms. The pile included bills for telephone, cell, electricity, cable television, Internet, and credit cards. She had no idea how much her tuition payments were or if they had been paid for this term. Those bills also had always gone directly to her father.

She picked up the late notice for her car payment. If she sold the car for enough to pay off the loan, she would eliminate that payment as well as insurance, gasoline, and parking costs. Jessica slid the pile of bills into a flat row and picked out the American Express and Visa envelopes. Without money to spend downtown or out in Schaumburg at the mall, would it really matter if she didn't have transportation? She set those two envelopes, unopened, on top of the bill from the insurance company.

Rifling through the bills from the utility companies, she added the phone bill to the pile of suddenly unnecessary expenses. She would rather give that up than her cell. The cable television bill got added to the I-can-live-without-it pile. The bill for broadband Internet stayed with the electric and cell phone envelopes — giving that up would make research more difficult. One by one, she opened the bills and entered the amounts into a spreadsheet on her computer.

Even with all her sacrifices — giving up car, telephone, cable, and shopping — Jessica didn't see how she could manage on less than eight hundred a month plus whatever she needed for tuition and books. One elbow on the black lacquered desktop, she leaned her forehead on the heel of her palm and stared at the computer screen. She would have to work full-time to earn enough to cover basic living expenses and tuition. "How the hell am I supposed to find time to keep up with school if I have to put in forty hours a week at some menial job?" Neither the computer nor the stack of bills offered an answer.

A tear rolled down her cheek, and Jessica caught it with the back of her hand. Her father's death threatened to destroy everything she had worked so hard on for the past three years. With a doctorate in psychology, she planned to make a name for herself in academic circles, doing cutting edge research on depression.

Jessica let loose a string of expletives and immediately covered her mouth, grateful no one could hear her cursing her father for not making more sensible investments. She closed her eyes, remembering when he quit his job to concentrate on day trading. She would come home from school to hear him brag about making thousands of dollars in the stock market in a single day. Her weekends at home invariably led to shopping excursions with her mother. Reveling in their new luxurious lifestyle, Lenora introduced Jessica to designer fashion, high-end furniture, exotic foods and more.

Pushing away from her desk and her memories, Jessica looked around at the black leather sofa and chairs, the carved, lacquered tables, brass lamps, and Bose sound system. She had acquired most of the hand-carved, Asian-style furniture since her mother missed a curve at a hundred and sixty miles an hour and crashed her new Ferrari into a concrete wall. The high-end furniture, designer shoes, and new jewelry hadn't closed the hole in Jessica's life that her mother left behind. Still, though they provided no solace for her grief, she had become rather accustomed to luxuries. And even if she readjusted to a more plebeian lifestyle, she still had no way of supporting herself.

Chapter Two

"I'm afraid I have all the T.A.s and R.A.s that I need for this term, Jessica." Professor Bob Clement leaned back in the large purple chair that barely held his impressive girth. The man stood six foot, four inches tall and his belly spilled over his thighs when he sat. "You should have come to me at the beginning of the term. I would have liked to have you on the team. The work you've done on your thesis shows a keen understanding of the role neurotransmitters play in triggering chronic depression." He brought the chair back down so he could fold his hands together on his office supply store desk calendar. "Besides, I thought you had the means to finance your education without subsidies from the University."

"I thought so, too." Jessica wanted to slip off her leather pumps and rub her tired toes. It had taken her nearly forty-five minutes to walk from her apartment. The brisk autumn wind had turned her cheeks red and made her nose runny. She resisted sniveling. "But my circumstances have changed rather drastically."

Professor Clement pulled on his black beard speckled with grey. "Most faculty select the students who will work for them during the fall term in the summer. The only person who might, and I empathize might, be in a position to add a student is the department chair."

Jessica cringed. That creep?

"And, while I wouldn't recommend that you change advisors this late in the process, if you need financial assistance, Professor Lawrence may be your only option for getting onboard as an assistant." He leaned his forearms on the desk. "Shame, really. Your interests have dovetailed so nicely with my research. I'll write you a nice recommendation, of course." He chewed on his lower lip. "Not that my support will carry much weight with Lawrence."

Continue Reading

Buy it in Print
978-1-937471-91-0
from Create Space

or Amazon
http://tinyurl.com/BrokeninPrint
or
E-Book
978-1-937471-90-3